MW01128935

# HEY, COACH!

## JEFF DUDAN

Copyright © 2015 The Will to Win Media Group, LLC

All rights reserved.

ISBN: 1511990570

ISBN-13: 978-1511990578

# RECOMMENDATIONS

"I would highly recommend Hey, Coach! to any current or "soon-to-be" volunteer youth sports coach. In today's "win-at-all-cost" youth sports culture that has become more about the coach's record than the kids, Jeff Dudan presents a much needed gut check on the true purpose of coaching and specific ways a coach can make an indelible impression on his or her player's lives."

—Brian Sanders
President & COO
i9 Sports Corporation

"As a professional athlete for 20 years, I can look back and see how instrumental coaches and mentors have been in my life, and using sports as a vehicle, helped shape me into who I am today. Now with young children of my own, I see the importance of the connection between coaches and children, and the opportunity to make an impact. Hey, Coach! lays out a framework to do just that, and I recommend it to anyone who wants to make the most out of the coaching opportunity."

—Christian Vande Velde
Professional Road Racing Cyclist
International Cycling Correspondent

"Hey, Coach! is a book about how to step up with confidence to volunteer to coach kids sports and along the way teach them life lessons. As a business leader and executive coach, I found the book's teachings to also be extremely valuable for adults in their working roles as part of a team or the team's manager/coach. This book contains transformational lessons that can be used for all ages and in any team environment!"

—Dave Zerfoss
  Former President, Husqvarna NA
  CEO, The Zerfoss Group
  Chair, Vistage International

"Jeff Dudan nails it when it comes to youth sports in America today. He brings an honest approach of the struggles most youth sport coaches face on a daily basis. Jeff's view on leadership and character is refreshing and inspiring. Hey, Coach! is a must read for any coach or parent looking to help young athletes through youth sports."

—Jeremy Martin
  Founder
  Ultimate Athlete

"Jeff understands the purpose driven role of the privilege of coaching young kids. He grabs the hearts of parents, coaches, former players and all of us who had those moments we want back so we can make things right – yet generously gifts us with those memories that fill our hearts with the joy of when we did the right thing. Perhaps a 'Must Read' – No – a 'Required Read' - for Youth Sports Coaches and Parents."

—Ed Kelley
Friend, Fellow Entrepreneur and Always a Coach
Former CEO, DigitalSports, Inc.
Pioneer Cofounder, Jiffy Lube

A page turner from beginning to end, this book is for coaches of all type. "Hey, Coach" is full of important ideas for both the athletic and business fields. It will simultaneously remind you of cherished memories and special characters in your life while illuminating important leadership lessons you can use today. This book is destined to become a classic.

—Joseph Hewitt
Founding Member, MedGift, LLC

# DEDICATION

To our starting five:

Jeff, Traci, Zack, Maelee and Jackson

Our lives represent our conversations with the universe. Every interaction creates a ripple in someone else's world and becomes a permanent part of their experience, and their story.

*Jeff Dudan*

# CONTENTS

# CHAPTER 1:
# THE LOSING STREAK

The other team: 7.

Matt's team: zip.

And here they were, two outs, nobody on base, bottom of the fifth. One more inning and the Bearcats, Matt's team of 10-year-olds, was going home with another loss. Two games into the season, and two games into a losing streak.

*It's going be a long season,* Matt thought as he stood along the first base line, trying to wear his game face and encourage this bunch of kids he had inherited from his buddy Scott. *Probably finagled that job transfer out of state just to get away from this team.*

Parents sitting in the bleachers and folding chairs beside the dugout were no longer clamoring for runs. The Bearcats needed way too many at this point. In fact, they were just a few runs away from the Mercy Rule; for kids this age, being down ten runs in the fifth inning meant game over.

As quiet as it was on Matt's side, high voices from the other team's dugout kept up a steady stream of chatter—theoretically aimed at encouraging their pitcher, but more than likely intended to rattle Matt's batters.

"One more out!"

"Send 'em home!"

Number 21 definitely looked rattled. He was short and spindly, his batter's helmet oversized above his narrow shoulders. His name was Luke, and so far today he'd struck out twice and contributed a couple of errors at third base. He had delivered about the same results during the first game of the season, which the Bearcats lost 9-2.

"Come on, Luke!" Matt called out in what he hoped was his most encouraging voice. "Let's get something started here. Base hit, buddy, base hit. You can do it!"

Luke glanced over, his mouth set in a grim line that looked to Matt not so much like determination, but like defeat. Matt wouldn't have been surprised to see the little boy drop his bat and slink away.

Instead, Luke did the next best thing: He swung for the fences—at a ball that came across the plate closer to his ankles than his knees.

The inning was over.

### 

John heard the familiar sounds of children playing baseball near the edge of the park—cheers, lots of chatter, the occasional crack of an aluminum bat against a ball. The sound called to him; in his younger days, he had spent many a perfect spring day in a ball park coaching his son and the neighborhood kids playing the all-American pastime. Volunteer coaching was one of the things John missed most about the old days.

Those days are over, he reminded himself. My kid's grown. House is empty. Grandkids are competing in robotics. Everything's different.

He looked down at his companion, a twelve-year-old Schnauzer whose hobble was even more arthritic than John's. "How about it, Buster? Where there's baseball, there must be bleachers. Let's take a rest before we head home."

Buster turned his panting snout in John's direction. His muzzle was as gray as John's own hair, but his eyes were still bright.

"I'm going to take that as a yes," John said, and turned down a gravel path through the trees toward the familiar sounds of an early spring baseball game.

Lost in thought since leaving his house a half-hour ago, John had marched all the way through the small town's business district, past the small college and the library and the gift shop and the old-fashioned ice cream parlor. He had made it well into the park at the edge of town before it occurred to him he had to turn around and walk the same distance back to the house. He still had the energy for the return trip— although home was no particular draw for him right now— but he wasn't sure about Buster, who was heavier around the middle than John.

A little breather was just what they needed.

This ball park looked a tad more ragged than the big new park on the other side of town. There was only one field, the bleachers were wooden and there were no concession stands, John realized as he came through a wooded stretch into the clearing. The chain link fence surrounding the field sagged in places and had rusted in a few others. And almost nobody was sitting on the bleachers—the parents on both sides had lined the fence with those folding chairs people carried around in bags. On the nearby sidewalk, younger children were drawing on the concrete with chalk. A friendly-looking Lab, whose leash was wrapped around the base of a dogwood tree whose blooms were still hanging on, thumped his tail heavily on the bare ground when John and Buster passed nearby.

Yep, John thought, things haven't changed much from the old days when I coached Little League.

John picked a spot on the near-empty bleacher behind the team wearing dark blue and red. Buster settled into the dust at his feet and immediately fell asleep. The Schnauzer would be snoring loudly before long.

John studied the team in blue and red. *My team,* he decided, since he'd picked the bleacher behind their dugout. *Runty little bunch,* he thought, *and not really into the game.* One of their own was at bat, but nobody was paying attention— except for the young coach, who was aggressively calling out encouragement to the scrawny kid whose batting helmet looked like it had been designed for someone twice his size.

The kid struck out—a pitiful effort. The ball came across the plate so low he would've needed a golf club to get to it.

Apparently, it was the third out, as the other team ran back to their dugout, whooping and hollering like a bunch of banshees. The team directly in front of John—the Bearcats, according to their uniforms—listlessly took up their positions in the field. The kid who thought he was playing golf, John noticed, played third base, a position that typically needed a good arm. John wondered if Golf Boy had a good arm; his gut told him no. The kid looked tentative and unsure of himself.

"One more inning," muttered a bored parent in a folding chair to John's right.

"How far up on us are they?" asked the guy next to him.

"Seven runs. Somebody needs to put this one out of its misery."

"Hey, Coach!" someone else shouted. "Let's get some outs, how 'bout it?"

A young woman with a baby in her lap shushed him, and people settled into a soft buzz of conversation about anything other than the game.

So it was a rout. John wasn't surprised.

Buster started snoring. A little girl about six years old came up, sat down in the dirt beside him and watched him snore.

"He's funny," the little girl said.

"He's old," John said. "We get funny when we get old."

The little girl stared at him solemnly, then nodded. "Yeah, my granddaddy's funny sometimes. Can I pet him? Will he bite me?"

"Nah. Buster doesn't have enough teeth to bite."

Giggling, the little girl scooted closer to the Schnauzer and patted him firmly on the head. Buster stopped snoring long enough to snuggle against her, then fell back asleep.

John turned his attention back to the field. The pitcher, a lanky kid with long curly hair poking through the back of his cap, had a little more promise. The kid pitched a couple across the plate. He had a pretty good arm for the age of this team—around nine years old, John speculated, based not just on their size but on their lack of physical grace and control.

The batter got a piece of the ball, and it scooted toward third base, where it should've been an easy catch for Golf Boy. Didn't happen. The ball rolled into the outfield and got lost in the weeds long enough for the batter to take second base. The other dugout erupted in cheers.

As the other team racked up another couple of runs, John began to wonder how the Bearcats had managed to get the other team out in the first five innings. He studied the coach, a young guy, no more than thirty-five, who looked like a classic baseball player—not very tall, stocky and broad-shouldered, square-jawed, the kind of leg muscles that said he could eat up the yards when he ran.

Yet despite his apparent athleticism, he looked completely out of his element, like he had no idea what to do other than cheer his team on with the expected platitudes.

Although the pitcher continued to do a pretty good job, the outfield was no help at all. They fumbled and stumbled their way through another run—three in all this inning—and two more outs, and the Bearcats were up again. Some of them didn't seem to know the basics; a few were clearly unfocused. The Bearcats, John decided, had a long, dismal season ahead of them.

"What'd ya expect?" groused the man nearest to John, loud enough for his voice to carry to the dugout. "Can't let a girl do your pitching."

"Oh, hush!" snapped a nearby mother. "She's the best player on the team."

A couple of other parents snickered.

"Oh, please!" replied the original grouser.

So the coach not only had a problem with his players, he had a problem with parents who didn't know any better than to take shots at the kids, especially if they might be in earshot. John had no patience for parents like that.

Shaking his head in disapproval, John looked toward the dugout. Sure enough, now that she was a little closer, it was easy to see the pitcher was a girl. And contrary to what the loud-mouthed guy in the red chair said, she was better than some of the others on the team. Sure, she needed some instruction—they all seemed to—but she showed signs of having the basic skill, maybe even some raw talent, to work with.

For the Bearcats, the bottom of the inning was short, and the game ended quickly.

Visitors 10, Bearcats 0 … by the mercy rule.

Still, by the time it was over, John found himself caught up in this team. They were cute kids, and some of them seemed so tense and beaten down he just wanted to corral them all for a little pep talk. They needed something, or somebody, to remind them they were kids and this was a game.

Parents started folding up their chairs and shoving them into their shoulder-sling bags. One young mother, who had a big smile despite the weary look in her eyes, pulled a rolling cooler up to the chain-link fence. After giving Golf Boy a quick hug, she started handing out drinks to the kids and the three coaches, who were standing around. John thought they looked as ineffective as the kids looked on the field. With this bunch leading the charge, these poor kids didn't stand a chance.

Finally, the first-base coach John had been eyeing stepped up, called the kids into a circle and just stood there, looking down at them.

### 

*Now what?* Matt wondered.

He looked down at the kids who should've been looking up to him. A few were clearly expecting some words that would somehow make sense of the beat down they had just endured. A few, like that poor kid Luke, were so disheartened they could only stare at their feet. Others looked either bored or discouraged and a couple of kids weren't even paying attention. They were horsing around—splashing bottled water and playfully knocking one another around—or standing at the fence talking to their parents. Matt wondered if they would even bother to come back for game three.

*You have to get control of this,* Matt ordered himself.

But how? Was this supposed to be a pep talk? A scolding? Matt tried to remember how his own high school coach might have handled the situation and realized there was no help there—his old coach would have reamed them out, using language that wasn't appropriate for a bunch of nine- and ten-year-olds.

"Okay, kids, listen up!" he said, raising his voice and settling on what he hoped was a tough tone. "You've gotta play like you want to win."

A couple of the players cocked their heads and looked confused. Matt realized he didn't even know their names. *How had he let himself get pulled into this at the last minute?*

"Do you?" he asked, a little more forcefully. "Do you want to win?"

One of the bigger kids rolled his eyes, as if to say, *Well, duh.* Matt felt his frustration grow. It was like these kids knew as well as he did he really wasn't prepared to coach them. His jaw tightened.

"Then you're going to have to do better than this," he said, his voice rising another notch. "This is our second big loss of the season, and I know you can do better."

*Do I really?* Matt wondered.

Rec center baseball wasn't known for attracting the town's best players anyway—those kids played tournament ball, had better equipment and better ball parks.

*Better coaches*, Matt needled himself.

But even in rec ball, the Bearcats were sort of the bottom of the rung—the ragtag leftovers who hadn't made it onto a team early in the process of selection. Small kids, those who weren't necessarily built for speed or strength, uncoordinated kids who probably had plenty of gifts, just maybe not in sports. A few who had missed skills day, so nobody had a clue how well they could play. In other words, kids nobody expected to do well.

Yet somehow Matt was supposed to make their parents happy and win baseball games.

Was it even possible, he wondered, to make this work?

*I don't even know exactly what I'm supposed to be doing with these kids,* he suddenly realized. Certainly not turning them into star athletes, he hoped, growing more peeved by the minute he'd gotten himself into this predicament in the first place…. all because he wanted to do a favor for his best friend.

And he couldn't forget Traci, his wife, who coaxed him by reminding him their two-year-old, Maelee, would be ready to play in a few years. "Don't you want to be involved when she's that age, Matt? Be there to look out for her? Wouldn't it be good to go ahead and get some experience now?"

Irritated with himself for caving to the pressure from Scott and Traci, Matt turned his attention back to his team of losers.

"The problem is, you're just not paying attention," he barked, his irritation getting the better of him. "You're out there daydreaming! So you don't even know when the ball is coming your way. If you do manage to get your hands on it, you drop it."

He glanced at the parents who were lining the fence. Some of them were nodding their agreement. A couple had their arms crossed over their chests, glaring at him, whether because he was criticizing their kids or because they held him responsible for the second loss of the season, Matt couldn't be sure. Other parents looked bored; they were ready to go home. And that edged Matt's irritation in the direction of anger. Maybe if these parents cared a little more, their kids wouldn't be out here making such a lame effort.

"And the way you run!" he continued. You can't expect to win with an effort like that! Can you?"

Nobody said a word.

"Well, can you?"

A few of them mumbled, "No, Coach."

"Of course not! You've got to give it one hundred percent!"

Then he launched into the same kind of play-hard tirade his old high school coach had been known for. He knew the kids weren't listening, but isn't that what he'd agreed to do—keep them in line and motivate them to win? Yet there didn't seem to be a future athlete in the whole bunch. What in the world was he supposed to do with them?

Mid-tirade, he glanced again in the direction of the restless parents. Without missing a beat in his heated speech to the players, he caught sight of an old guy sitting on the bleachers with a tired old Schnauzer at his feet. A grandfather to one of the kids, no doubt. The old geezer stared at Matt and, for a moment, Matt felt certain he could read the old man's thoughts.

You're getting it all wrong, kid.

The message came through so loud and clear Matt wondered for a moment if the old man had actually spoken the words.

Worst of all, Matt knew it was true. And if he couldn't figure out how to get it right, these kids would be the ones to pay the price.

What in the world am I doing here?

## Coach's Rule #1

*Answer this question first: "Why am I doing this?"*

# CHAPTER 2:
# WHY BOTHER?

The address of the new prospect for Matt's small remodeling company was on one of the nicer streets in Stonefield, a quiet, tree-lined street of Craftsman bungalows built about a century earlier and often in need of repairs.

From talking to the guy on the phone, Matt knew this wasn't a big job, but he hoped he could nail it. The exposure would be just the ticket for getting more business in this nice older neighborhood, where homeowners might have more discretionary income for remodeling projects. And with a small crew of young, mostly inexperienced laborers, Matt wanted to do this for them as much as he wanted to do it for himself.

He could always go back to doing it solo; in many ways it had been a whole lot less aggravation and stress in those days than being the boss. But he liked the idea of providing jobs, helping these younger guys start to make their own way in the world—the way his dad had done for him when he was straight out of college a dozen years ago.

Matt had lived in Stonefield his whole life, which should've been a plus for a small business owner. But he knew a lot of the long-time residents of this small North Carolina town still saw him as the son of Irene and Matthew, Sr. Things changed slowly in this small Southern town. However, despite knowing the town as well as he knew his own house, Matt didn't recognize the name of this new prospect—John Holdridge—and concluded he must be new in town.

The house was tucked back on a deep, wooded lot. With its cedar shakes and dormered roof shading a wide front porch, the two-story house wasn't big, but the design was a classic. And because of the neighborhood, Matt knew it must've cost Holdridge a pretty penny. As Matt pulled his pickup into the driveway, he caught a glimpse of a wheelchair ramp on the back of the house. Ah, that must be why John Holdridge had selected him; Matt had started to develop a specialty niche with older homeowners who needed to remodel for accessibility.

As Matt got out of his truck, the front door opened and an older man came out onto the porch and down the front steps. Tall and lean with only a little bit of stiffness in his gait, John Holdridge seemed to have no trouble getting around. Matt approached the homeowner with his clipboard when a little dog began to step gingerly down the front steps. That was when Matt recognized his new prospect—the grandfatherly guy who'd been watching the game from the bleachers the other night with his Schnauzer.

*Great. Just great.* Matt was already a loser in this guy's eyes.

After they shook hands and exchanged a formal introduction, the homeowner led Matt around to the side of the house and pointed to the ramp.

"I want that removed," he said brusquely, then walked up the ramp with no further explanation.

Surprised, Matt made a note and followed John inside.

"I want this island ripped out," he said, pointing to a granite-topped island in the kitchen that had been custom-built to accommodate wheelchairs. "Want a new one, standard counter height."

Again, John didn't wait for further conversation, but walked quickly through a cozy—if slightly old-fashioned—family room, down a hallway and into the master bedroom. He pointed to the master bath, which was equipped with a high-end wheelchair-accessible sink and shower.

"And get that out of here. Just give me a tub. Nothing fancy. Just a plain old tub." John turned quickly away. "And all those hand bars. Want those out, too."

Matt's first inclination was to tell John he might consider keeping things as they were. Accessibility upfits, Matt knew, would command a premium price for the right buyer if, or when, Holdridge decided to sell the house. Stonefield, with its picturesque, small-town feel, its mild Southern weather and the nearby big city with so many cultural amenities, attracted a lot of newcomers, including retirees from the Northeast. Plenty of those retirees would be looking for these amenities over the next decade.

But something in John's demeanor—his clipped language, his gruff tone, the firm set to his jaw—told Matt to keep his mouth shut. This was not a client who was looking for input.

As they headed toward the back deck, Matt asked questions about the details he would need to know before pricing the project. They paused at the kitchen island while Matt made a few more notes. Then he eased into a little small talk. His dad had always taught him people did business with people, not companies.

"What brought you to Stonefield?" he asked with a smile.

"Oh, you know…retirement…new scenery." John leaned down to pick up the old dog. Matt noted the old man seemed surprisingly limber and strong for his age. "New England winters are hard on some old dogs, you know. How about you? This your hometown?"

He seemed to be relaxing now the business was out of the way.

Matt nodded. "Four generations."

"How long you been coaching?"

Matt felt his smile freeze. The old man did remember him. "Not long. But that's pretty obvious, I suppose."

John chuckled. "Well, it looks like you don't have a lot to work with. I guess the best players get snapped up by the tournament teams or the guys running the league. Funny how that happens."

Nothing in John's tone sounded condescending or judgmental, and Matt felt himself thawing. "That's true. In rec league, we get a lot of kids who aren't even thinking about playing sports in middle or high school." He was surprised to hear himself adding, "But don't they deserve to have a good experience too?"

"Sure they do. Kids need the opportunity to learn and have fun even if they don't appear to be naturally athletic or competitive…at this point anyway." John gestured at the coffee pot on the counter, a question on his face. When Matt shook his head, John pulled one mug out of the dish drainer and poured a cup for himself. "Besides, you never can tell. It's easy to pigeonhole a kid who doesn't look like an athlete. But you can't write a kid off. You can't judge a kid's heart, how a player will come through for the team when it counts, or how they may develop a love for a sport that leads them to put the work in to get considerably better over time."

Matt filed that thought away. His initial reaction was it was an overly optimistic notion. But then he remembered how his young crew members surprised him on the job. Some turned out to be the ones with the best ideas for solving problems or the most willing to work. Maybe this old guy was right; John Holdridge had a lot he could teach Matt.

As they headed out toward his truck, Matt said, "You must like kids' sports if you stopped by last night. You come across to me as someone who has done some coaching in your time."

"You're right, and I do. Honestly last night I was just looking for a place to sit down for a few minutes before we headed for home," the old guy said. "Can I ask you a question?"

"Sure."

"So, what's your strategy going to be for this group of kids now that you know what you are dealing with in terms of players?"

"My strategy?"

"Yeah, do you have any thoughts on what success could be for this team, for these kids, and how you can get them from where they are today, to a better place on the last day of the season?"

Matt felt like he'd just been handed a pop quiz and he'd never even read the assignment. He must've had a deer-in-the-headlights look because John smiled.

"Here's another way to say it, coach. Based on what I saw yesterday, this group is not likely to walk away with the championship trophy. So if that is the case, how are you going to create some success for them in other ways they can feel good about, and maybe learn something meaningful along the way?" John asked. "How many different ways can you dream up that would feel like a win for your kids, even if the scoreboard said something else?" The words were spoken gently, but Matt suddenly realized John was describing a key responsibility of a head coach—to make this experience positive for kids who some people expected to end up at the bottom of the heap. "I...well, now that you ask...I suppose I ought to be ashamed to admit it, but I'm not sure I *have* a strategy. I mean, except to find a way to win a few games between now then, maybe." And winning, he could see, might be a long shot for this particular group of kids. Where did that leave him—and them?

John smiled and shrugged. "Well Matt, being an old ball coach myself for many years, it took me several years to figure out I needed a strategy." John let the comment hang in the air for a moment, then added. "Actually, that's wrong. You need two strategies. Any idea what they might be?"

Matt smiled back, but thought it was a strange question. After all, this was only ten year old baseball. Right?

John took a long swallow of his coffee while Matt wrestled with an answer, which John clearly expected.

Then John said, "You look like a ball player; what do you think is going on with the team?"

Matt tossed his clipboard through the open window of his truck. "I...well...I don't know. First I would say we just don't have the athletes the other teams have. And honestly, I am not really clicking with my assistant coaches; we're just not on the same page. But the biggest surprise for me is the parents. I can't believe the junk I'm hearing from the stands. I know people want their kids to compete but it seems a bit much to me...at least at this age." John was grinning from ear to ear, as if he was reliving a happy memory from another time. "Now that sounds familiar. You have to get your people right, Matt. You always have to start with a people strategy. People are the first thing. You either manage the people, or they will manage you right into the looney bin, or maybe into an early retirement from youth coaching."

Yep. Matt was immediately aware he was in over his head coaching this team and sinking fast.

As he struggled to think through the advice John had thrown out, the old man threw him another curve ball.

"How about you, then?" John said. "Coaching kids is quite a commitment of time and energy. Why are you doing this?"

Despite his self-doubt in the aftermath of last night's loss, Matt felt on more solid ground with this question. "My little girl is two and, well, to be honest, my wife wanted me to get into coaching now. So I'll be ready when Maelee is ready."

"That's a good enough reason, I suppose," John said, although Matt had the strongest feeling the old guy didn't think it was a very good reason at all. "Having a significant 'why' is important, isn't it?"

"Sure," Matt replied.

John Holdridge struck Matt as awfully philosophical about something as ordinary as kids' baseball. Maybe that came with the territory for old guys with too much time on their hands.

John offered his hand, and they shook. "So you'll get me an estimate?"

"You bet. I can drop it off tomorrow." Matt hopped into his truck.

"Sounds good."

As John backed away from the truck, Matt said, "Drop by the ball field anytime. We have our third game Saturday at two o'clock."

John nodded. "Thanks. Might just do that."

Matt backed down the driveway, thinking. *Just what I need, another witness.*

### 

All the way home that night, John Holdridge's "why" question kept popping into Matt's mind, the way it had all day as he'd visited job sites and talked to his crew supervisors.

*Why was he doing this?*

*Why take on this hassle for a bunch of unmotivated kids who don't seem to care at all?*

*Why spend time that he, as the owner of a struggling small business, couldn't afford to take away from his work or his family, just to lead a losing team?*

*Was this about him and what he wanted to get out of it, or was this about what the kids could walk away with at the end of the season?*

*Or some of both? Maybe he did need a people strategy, starting with one for himself!*

Matt's head was spinning as he walked through the back door just in time to help Traci put Maelee to bed for the night. He was worn out, but he enjoyed taking ten minutes to listen to Traci tell their daughter a story as she snuggled under the covers, a little plate of cut-up bananas on the bedside table. Matt smiled. It was their little family joke. Could Maelee finish her banana before she fell asleep? Usually, the answer was no. As he watched the familiar scene, Matt couldn't imagine loving anything more than he loved Traci and Maelee. Sometimes he resented the fact he worked so hard and had so little time to spend with them.

*So why is it,* he asked himself yet again, *you're taking more time away from them to coach a team of misfits and leftovers?*

After Maelee was in bed, Matt went into the third bedroom he had converted into his home office to check his email and work on the estimate for John Holdridge. The room could use a little of his own remodeling skills—it was crammed with mismatched file cabinets, and his desk with a hutch covered most of the only window. The old hardwood floors were scarred, and the closet door never closed because it wasn't quite square. Some efficient built-ins, some track lighting and a few electrical upgrades would be a big improvement. The place could use a coat of paint, too—the walls had faded to a dingy off-white, and the scuffed baseboards still had the six layers of paint from when he and Traci had bought the house as a fixer-upper four years earlier.

Matt told himself one day he would have the time—and the spare cash—to get around to fixing up his office. But not before he fixed up the kitchen and the master bath for Traci.

As he did the calculations of materials and time to work up the estimate for John Holdridge, Matt also questioned why he insisted on working so hard to make a go of his little company. That was easier to answer than the question about coaching, he told himself, as Traci came into his office with a plate of reheated dinner. He worked this hard for Traci, who was smart and funny and beautiful and sweet. He did it for Maelee, a little redhead like her mom, who was beginning to show all the signs of independence and intelligence Matt loved in Traci. He did it because he wanted a good future for his family, just the way his dad had done it for him.

He even did it because the business and his own abilities were his legacy from his dad.

"Hard day?" Traci placed the plate on the desk beside his laptop, kissed him on the cheek and dropped into the old recliner beside his desk.

"Not bad." Matt opened his inbox as he started to devour his dinner. Four emails were from team parents. "A new client, maybe."

"Can you handle that with your schedule?"

He smiled, nodded and opened one of the emails from a parent. The dad wasn't happy with him. The language wasn't kind. Matt closed it; he would deal with that later. He opened a second email from another parent. More choice words.

"I'll manage," he said. "How was your day?"

She closed her eyes and pulled the lever on the old recliner to raise her legs. "Not bad. Maelee was cranky all day. I didn't get my workout in—again. And I saw Sarah Kate Lessing at the grocery store."

He decided not to open the other two parent emails. He wanted to enjoy a few minutes with his wife. "Who?"

"Sarah Kate, Ron Lessing's wife. Ron was the EMT who died last fall trying to get the girl out of the car on the freeway."

Matt remembered now. The girl's car was on fire. She was trapped. Just a high school kid. The EMT had insisted on working to release her long after he was ordered to back away. The car exploded. Neither Ron nor the girl made it. The news left the entire town heartbroken and in shock.

"How's Sarah Kate doing?" he asked.

"She's okay. About like you might expect. She said you're coaching her son."

"Really? Who's that?"

"His name is Luke."

Of course, the skinny little kid with the sad look in his eyes. The one who couldn't hit, and couldn't field a ball if his life depended on it.

"Sarah Kate said she doesn't understand why, but playing on this team seems to mean the world to Luke. She...she knows he isn't much of a player."

Matt nodded and grinned wryly. "That's an understatement."

"That's why Sarah Kate said she's so grateful you're the coach—a lot of coaches wouldn't put the time in with him...she seems to think you will."

Matt winced, thinking of his harsh words to the kids the other night after their loss. Maybe he wasn't such a prize as a coach.

Two hours later, after Traci had gone to bed and Matt was finishing up the estimate for John Holdridge, he thought about John's question again. *Why are you doing this?*

Luke's face popped into his mind. And Sarah Kate, just hoping Matt would invest some time in Luke, at a time when Luke needed it most.

Why? Matt knew he had his answer. It's because of kids like Luke—and what it could mean to Luke at this point in his life. And the more he thought about it, all kids really need adults who are willing to invest in their lives. That felt right.

Now that he had his 'why,' Matt knew he still had to figure out how.

## Coach's Rule #2

*Do it for the kids, not the parents, not for the love of the sport, and not for your own ego.*

*It's about the kids—-all of them.*

# CHAPTER 3:
# BAD BEHAVIOR, BAD PERFORMANCE

Matt went to the next practice fired up. His new awareness he was in this for the kids had inspired a new level of commitment from him to turn the team around, get the kids under control for their own good, starting right now.

It was going to be great!

The kids straggled in, some of them clearly apathetic and some of them erupting with uncontained energy. Five minutes before practice was supposed to start, one of the assistant coaches texted him with a lame excuse for missing tonight's practice. So Matt was going to be one assistant short.

"Okay, team, bring it in," Matt called out over the noise of the kids.

A couple of the players came forward—the pitcher, Luke, and a couple of other boys seemed to have more focus than many of the players. But most of them continued to horse around and giggle. One kid just sat in the dirt, drawing circles with the sewn edge of his glove; he never even looked up when Matt spoke.

Their parents settled into their folding chairs and stared at the chaos.

All except Sarah Kate, the young widow his wife had mentioned to him. When she saw most of the kids were still bouncing around, she quietly made her way onto the field with Will and Josh, the remaining assistant coaches, and helped them herd the boys into the circle around Matt.

Thanking her with a nod of his head, Matt looked down at his team and wondered where to start.

"Okay, Bearcats, listen up! We have a big game coming up in two days," he said, extremely conscious of the fact about a dozen parents had very critical eyes on him. "So let's get ready. I want...uh, we're going to practice hitting and throwing the ball, okay? Half of you grab a bat and go with Josh. The rest of you, partner up and get out on the field. Will and I are going to come around, take a look at how you're doing and give you some pointers."

Was that as lame as it sounded?

Apparently, it was. Even the kids didn't move, just stared up at him as if to say, *That's it? That's all you got?*

Matt clapped his hands together once. "Come on! Pair up! Let's get going!"

The result was not what Matt had envisioned. Instead of two rows of kids facing each other across an expanse of outfield, throwing balls back and forth to a partner, the field erupted in chaos, with kids in groups of twos and fours throwing the ball in all directions. Only two of the kids had followed Josh.

Will came over and asked, "Is this what you had in mind?"

Matt had to laugh at himself. "No. I have to admit this isn't exactly what I envisioned."

Between the two of them, they brought a little more order to the field. They sent half the kids over to batting practice.

Within ten minutes, the others were doing a reasonable imitation of practicing their throw. The element of chaos didn't disappear completely, but it did become a little more like managed chaos.

Matt and Will walked the rows, giving pointers to the individual kids for about twenty minutes, then switched up the groups—a transition that took twice as long as it should have.

After Will had the new group under control, Matt went over to observe batting practice. It was dismal.

Matt was no pro, but even he could tell the batting stances were horrible. Some of the players were able to make contact with the ball. Most of them were wildly out of control. Luke seemed to flinch on every pitch which accounted for the fact he only swung at balls that were too low or too far outside.

Then there was the kid who had been drawing circles in the dirt. His name was Mason. He was a tall, strong-looking kid, but he seemed to inhabit another planet. No matter how Matt encouraged him, he refused to even take a cut at the ball. He just stood there, his stance perfect and his bat absolutely motionless.

Matt walked over to home plate. "Mason, I need you to take a swing, buddy. Okay?"

Mason stared down at the plate and nodded.

Matt took a step back and nodded to Josh, who was lobbing the balls to the plate.

For the fourth time, Mason settled into a perfect batting stance, his eyes riveted on the ball as it approached the plate. He made no attempt to hit the ball.

Matt pursed his lips. "Okay, next time, Mason. Let's give Ethan a shot now."

Seeming completely unfazed by his failure to perform, Mason walked away and sat in the dirt outside the dugout. During the rest of practice, he drew circles in the dirt.

When practice began to wind down, Matt noticed two of his players had made their way over to Mason and were hunkered down close to him. Mason edged away from them, and the two boys laughed.

Matt walked over. "Everything okay here?"

The two boys shrugged. One of them, Hunter, said, "Sure."

Matt looked down at Mason. "Mason? Everything okay here?"

Mason didn't look at him, but clutched his glove and stood up. "Okay. Yes, everything's okay here."

Mason walked hurriedly toward the dugout. Hunter and Ethan followed him; Matt heard them snickering. He wondered if there was more going on with Mason than just a kid who didn't like swinging a bat.

Sighing over what felt like a complete disaster of a practice, Matt reminded himself: Mason was his "why." And even if he didn't like the way they were acting, so were Hunter and Ethan.

But he still needed to figure out the "how"—soon.

As he gathered up his things in the dugout, Matt was hit by a revelation: He knew almost nothing about these kids—these young individuals—who were on his team. He had never asked them why they were playing, who their favorite players were, whether they had brothers and sisters, or if they played another sport—nothing. They were just kids to him, not real young people with personalities and motives and their own complicated set of life experiences.

He was telling himself these kids were his "why." Who was he kidding? He'd barely made an effort to figure out who these kids were.

### 

Sarah Kate draped the strap of her bag chair over her shoulder and resisted the urge to put her arm around Luke's shoulders until they were out of sight of the field. She tried to be sensitive to the fact when little boys reach a certain age the last thing they want is to have their mothers clinging to them in front of other kids.

"How are you enjoying baseball?" she asked.

Luke shrugged. "It's okay."

"You don't have to play, you know. Nobody's making you play." He had never wanted to play sports when Ron was alive—in fact, he was kind of a computer geek, when he didn't have his head stuck in a book. She doubted if baseball was something her son really was passionate about. And clearly, he was having no fun.

"Mo-o-om."

She almost smiled, amazed how good it felt just to hear him sounding so typically little boy. "I'm just saying."

"I told you. I wanna play."

Their new house was just a five-minute walk down a quiet street near the edge of the park. They had lived in a different neighborhood before Luke's father died, but Sarah Kate knew supporting them on her job as a teacher would require cutting back. Instead of spending her husband's life insurance to keep them afloat, she had invested the money, hoping it would be enough to pay for Luke's college one day. Then she sold their bigger house—the one she and Ron had owned since they were newlyweds—and bought a smaller house.

Sarah Kate had realized too late the move, so soon on the heels of losing his dad, had been like a second loss to her son. She sighed, certain it wouldn't be the last mistake she'd make as a single parent.

"So tell me what you like about being a Bearcat?" she said as their small two-bedroom house came into view.

He rolled his eyes at her.

She laughed and gave his shoulder a soft punch, the way she imagined a father might. *The way Ron would*, she thought, swallowing the lump in her throat, *if he could be here*. "Okay, okay."

As they turned up their front sidewalk, she said, "Your dad loved baseball. He always said he hoped one day you would take it up so you could do it together. He wanted to coach you." Luke looked down at his shoes. "Yeah? He said that?"

"Yep."

She unlocked the door and turned on the overhead light in the living room. As Luke headed down the hallway to his room, he called back, "The part I like is Taylor."

Taylor. The little girl who was the pitcher. Her son's first crush. Despite the tears that sprang to her eyes, Sarah Kate smiled and wished Ron were there to share the moment.

### 

Matt drove home from practice, equal parts discouraged about his team and disgusted with himself for being so unprepared to coach a bunch of kids. When he'd agreed to take on the role of coach, he'd felt confident he would know what to do and just wing it. After all, he'd played baseball from the time he was seven or eight all the way through high school. He'd been a pretty decent player, too. Not exactly a star, but a solid utility player. But coaching, it seemed, was above his pay grade.

All he could think about was how badly he'd already bungled the job. He didn't have a clue about these kids. He didn't know a thing about the kids' parents and their expectations. It made his head hurt.

As he was turning the corner onto Main Street, he spotted John Holdridge walking his dog. Matt tapped his horn and waved. John waved back, then motioned for him to pull over. Matt pulled into a spot at the curb and pushed the button to lower the passenger window. John walked over and leaned in.

"Hi, Mr. Holdridge."

"You're going to need to call me John if you're going to be working on my house, young man," John said with a hint of gruffness.

"Yes, sir, Mr. … John." He smiled. Despite the old guy's tone, Matt already suspected there was nothing gruff about John Holdridge. "So the bid suited you?"

"Yes, I think I can live with it. As long as we can get the work done soon."

"We can get out there the first of next week."

"Sounds good. Say, how's that team of yours doing?"

Matt chuckled. "Well, I don't think we're going to be in a pennant race this year."

John smiled. "Don't give up on 'em."

Matt wanted to say the team was more likely to give up on him. "No, I won't."

"Buster and I are thinking about coming out for the next game. "Great!" Matt said. "Say, you and Buster need a lift home?"

"No, no. It's good for us to keep moving, even if we aren't moving very fast."

As he drove off, Matt secretly hoped his new client would forget about the next game. He just couldn't see how it could be anything but humiliating.

### 

Matt's expectations for the third game of the season were not far off base.

In the first inning, Jackson and Zack got on base with ground balls; two worm-burners that each found their way through the infield. Runners on first and second, no outs. Matt was starting to feel a little bit of optimism as Brady stepped up to the plate. Brady jumped on the first pitch and lofted a lazy fly ball directly to the right fielder. Both runners tagged up. Jackson made it safely to third, but Zack got caught in a rundown between first and second base. Suddenly the Bearcats had two outs and a man on third. Jermaine, fourth in the lineup and a big, strong kid swung for the fence three times and struck out.

The bottom of the first was dismal. The other team manufactured three runs, with a little help from the Bearcat fielders. Matt realized they desperately needed a better catcher. Jermaine struggled to keep dirt balls in front of him and squeeze the ones that hit the mitt. Catching was not his thing. And Matt desperately needed help in the outfield. Easy fly balls just had to be outs. And few of them had any idea the correct base to throw the ball when they did manage to field it cleanly.

The second inning was a quick three up and three down for the Bearcats, followed in the bottom of the inning by two more runs for the other team. At which point Josh, his third base coach, lit into Luke for dropping a pop up while everyone was transitioning to the dugout.

"Come on, kid. That was an easy out! That ball fell right on you! All you had to do was—"

Matt stepped between Josh and Luke. "That's enough, Josh," he said quietly. "He knows he missed the ball," as Matt reached back and put his hand on Luke's shoulder.

"Yeah, well, he needs to—" Josh started to say.

Matt interrupted, "He feels bad enough already. He doesn't need to hear anything else." Josh, his face even redder now, despite the fact Matt had kept his comments low so no one else would hear, narrowed his eyes and stalked toward the dugout. As he passed, Matt added, "And by the way, his name is Luke. Not 'kid,' it's Luke."

"Whatever."

By the time Josh made it to the dugout, Matt realized Luke was still frozen, his eyes facing down. Matt knelt down in front of Luke and said, "We've all missed a pop up. You'll get it next time. Don't sweat it, just forget it. It's over." He wanted to hug the kid.

*Sometimes,* Matt told himself as he took up his position outside the dugout, *it's the coaches who need the coaching.* The third inning opened near the bottom of the hitting lineup—Luke. Terrific.

Luke usually looked intimidated or unsure of himself. Now, he looked terrified. Matt glared at Josh, hoping he could see the damage he'd done.

Luke took a half-hearted swing at the ball and caught just enough of it to dribble it into fair territory. It became a bunt, and Luke was out long before he made it to first base. The kids from the other dugout were snickering, and even the Bearcats' dugout was groaning just a bit.

"Come on, Coach!" came the cry from one of the parents behind him. "Get your act together!"

Matt cut his eyes in the direction of the criticism, but he couldn't tell which of the parents had spoken. As disappointed as he was in the caliber of play by these kids, the last thing he wanted was for them to feel the brunt of criticism and ridicule.

Luke pursed his lips and went back to the dugout dry-eyed. A lesser kid might've cried after two cringe-worthy plays in a row. Matt had to give him credit for that. The kid was growing on Matt.

The next batter, Eli, struck out but kept the ball alive through six pitches. Matt gave the boy a shout of encouragement as he ran back to the dugout with an incongruously big smile on his face. Smaller than most of the other boys with a full head of dark, loose curls, Eli was obviously out to enjoy the game whether he played well or not.

Gabe, another small kid and a lefty, managed a walk.

The final batter in the lineup was Mason.

"Here we go, Mason." Matt said as Mason switched his cap for a batting helmet, something Josh should have reminded him to do while Eli was at the plate. "You can do this,

Mason. Eyes on the ball, take a good cut. You've got this, pal."

*Right.*

Still, if Mason could just get on base and Gabe made it to second—they'd be back at the top of the line-up. Maybe they could get something going with two outs.

Mason settled into his nice looking stance with a natural ease that just didn't fit with the rest of his moves on the field. He leveled a menacing glare at the pitcher. Matt was impressed by the kid's presence at home plate; he could see the pitcher grow nervous facing Mason.

Those nerves showed on the first pitch. The ball hit the ground at Mason's feet. Mason didn't move a muscle. A few encouraging cheers came from the crowd. Still Mason remained motionless.

"Good eye, Mason!" Josh called from the third-base line.

"Way to watch it, Mason!" Matt added.

The second ball was high and to the outside. Ball two. Matt unobtrusively pumped his fist. Maybe this pitcher would walk Mason.

No such luck. After a little pep talk from the coach on the other side, the pitcher got his act together and threw three strikes. Mason's bat did not move from his right shoulder.

The cheers in the audience behind the Bearcats' dugout turned into a collective, audible sigh. All the cheers were from the other dugout and the fans on the other side.

The game went downhill from there. From his spot at third base, Luke dropped another ball, this one thrown to him from the outfield—a ball that could have been an easy out but turned into a run for the other team instead. Although he couldn't hear what was said, Matt could see Josh speaking to Luke through gritted teeth, and he was sure the assistant coach's words weren't encouraging. There was a scuffle in the dugout between Hunter, who seemed to see himself as the star of the team and therefore the one everybody ought to listen to, and Gabe, who had stumbled on the way to first base for the final out of the game. Luke, in the wrong place at the wrong time, ended up with a bloody nose. Somebody— nobody was sure who—pushed Taylor when she tried to step in and defend Gabe.

One way or the other, it seemed to Matt, everybody was behaving badly tonight.

The final score was 11-1. The sole run, thanks to Zack, who made it on base during the fourth inning, and Ethan, who batted him in.

### 

"Man, this hurts to watch," said the burly man next to John on the bleachers.

John nodded. "You got a kid out there?"

"Number 9. Zack."

"He's pretty good."

"Thanks. We were out of town and he missed skills day, so none of the coaches knew what he had. They passed on him and…" He sighed heavily. "I don't know if he's going to stick with this team. I mean, if he wants out, I'm not sure I'll make him stay. It's pretty rough."

"I can see how this could be real discouraging for a boy with some talent." John extended his hand. "I'm John."

"Charlie." They shook. "You got a kid out here, John?"

"No. Just looking for something to do on a Saturday afternoon. Me and Buster." He gestured toward the dog at his feet.

"Well, I'm sure the coaches will get things under control," Charlie said.

A father in a folding chair to their left snorted. "Somebody needs to kick this head coach in the can. He's doing nothing to turn this around!"

"He was a last-minute substitute," someone muttered. "I heard he played ball, but I'm not sure he knows a bat from a hockey stick."

Charlie spoke up, a slight edge to his voice. "Give him a chance. If he stepped up when he was needed, we need to cut him some slack while he works with our kids."

When the game was over and the other parents were putting away their chairs and their coolers and migrating toward the fence, John looked at Charlie. "I like your attitude."

"I just don't think this is all on the coach. Most of these kids are new to baseball." Charlie said. "The coaches are going to need some help with these kids if the team's going to stay out of the basement."

"You play?"

Charlie shrugged. "Oh, you know. A little here and there."

John read people pretty well, and he had a hunch Charlie's "a little here and there" represented a lot more playing time than most of the parents who were so busy trying to figure out who to blame.

When the post-game huddle was over, Charlie gave John a wave and walked over to rap knuckles with his son. They walked toward the parking lot, Charlie's big hand on Zack's shoulder as they talked.

John decided to hang out and speak to Matt before he and Buster walked home. Matt looked pretty downhearted when he exited the field.

"Tough game," John said.

Matt looked up and smiled wryly. "Kind of a disaster, I'd say."

"Well, they're young." John tugged on Buster's leash to rouse him from his nap, and they walked toward Matt.

"Yeah, they're doing the best they can, I suppose."

They reached the parking lot, where Matt threw a bag full of equipment into the back of his truck. "I'd like to give those parents some coaching, I can tell you that."

"Must be hard to hear all the criticism."

Matt shook his head. "What they say about me, I don't care about that. But they don't seem to realize those kids on the field hear them and soak up all their nasty remarks. The kids take it personally, even if I don't. They don't need their own parents ragging on them."

"Well said," John agreed. "You have your hands full with this group of parents. With what I am hearing in the stands, I can't imagine what is being said in the car on the way home from the game. As the first step in your people strategy, I suggest you address the parents and set clear expectations. Parents need to be partners with the coach in developing their kids, not antagonists."

Matt paused. "Expectations like what?"

"Well, for starters." John continued. "Talk about why you are doing this. If you have the right purpose, it should be something everybody can buy into and get behind. If not, at least they will know where you stand and what you are trying to do for their kids. Then, just layout some ground rules that make sense and reflect what kind of example parents should set for these kids, all of them, on both teams. And hey, you're the coach, so go with what you think matters. Remember, the coach defines the program. It's a perk that comes with the job anyway."

Matt smiled.

"So, I'll see your crew Monday morning?" John asked.

"We'll be there first thing."

As John and Buster walked away, Matt realized another truck was idling nearby. It was Josh. He started his engine slowly, waiting to see if Josh would approach him. When Josh made no move, Matt decided to take the bull by the horns. He pulled up next to Josh's truck, driver-side door to driver-side door.

"Something you want to say?" he asked, trying to keep his tone as non-confrontational as possible.

There was a moment of hesitation before Josh said, "Yeah. You've got no right to talk to me that way."

His tone was hostile, the tone of a belligerent adolescent.

"You were out of line with Luke."

"The kid's incompetent," Josh said. "He lost the game for us."

"There's plenty of room for blame to go around. But we're not going to play it that way with the kids. You understand?" Matt kept his own anger under tight control. "If anybody is at fault this early in the season, it's us."

"Speak for yourself, *Coach*." The final word came out like a sneer.

"Okay," Matt said. "I will. If anybody's at fault, it's me. The question is, are you going to be part of the problem or are you going to work with me to be part of the solution?"

"I don't know if you could find the solution with both hands."

"Maybe not. But that doesn't answer the question: Are you in or out?"

"Coach, *you* are the problem. Those useless kids are the problem. And I'm not going to hang around so you can yell at me because you don't have the guts to yell at them."

"Just so we're clear, then—you're quitting?"

Josh stared at him in disgust. "Yeah. I'm out of here. And I'm taking Henry with me." He roared off in his pickup.

Henry—a big-shouldered kid might've been a good contributor to the team, but Matt figured the Bearcats would survive losing father and son.

Matt sat there in his truck until his anger subsided. Josh might be right about Matt. Maybe he didn't know how to find the solution. *Maybe I am the problem*, he thought. But he would not do what Josh did and take it out on the kids. And he wouldn't let his assistant coaches do it, either.

### 

When he arrived home, Maelee had just fallen asleep and Traci had put her feet up for a few minutes before cleaning the kitchen. Matt gave her a kiss.

"How was the game?" she asked, stifling a yawn.

"Don't ask," he said. "Let's just say the streak continues and leave it at that."

Traci smiled sympathetically. "Sorry."

"How about yours?"

"Pretty good. Maelee's best friend has the sniffles, so I'm hoping Maelee doesn't wake up with them in the morning."

She reached over and began to knead his shoulders and neck. "Say, don't you have a new job starting Monday?"

"Yeah. A new guy in town." He groaned appreciatively as Traci began to loosen some of the knots in his shoulders. "Kinda weird. He's an old guy, but he wants to take out all the accessibility features in the house—ramp, walk-in shower, everything. I keep wanting to tell him those things could be worth money at resale time."

"What's his name? Do I know him?"

"Probably. Holdridge. John Holdridge."

Traci worked part-time in the registrar's office at the local college and seemed to know everybody. "Oh, no wonder. That's the Dean's dad."

Of course. Dean Andrew Holdridge. "Say, didn't his mom die recently?"

"That's right. About four months ago. His parents moved down here when his mom was diagnosed with ALS about a year ago."

"Ah. Makes sense John would want all the reminders of his wife's illness gone." He patted Traci's knee. "Okay, before you completely spoil me, I need to check my emails. Meet you back here in twenty?"

"It's a deal."

The first thing Matt saw was an email from Lonnie the assistant coach who had been a no-show for the last practice and tonight's game—and a good buddy of Josh's. He was resigning, too.

Matt slumped in his desk chair. Great. He had a team that didn't seem to have a clue, and he was down to one assistant coach.

And he'd thought it couldn't get any worse.

Suddenly irritated, as he remembered the way a handful of parents had been so vocal within earshot of kids who already felt bad about the game, Matt shot off a quick response to Lonnie, thanking him for the help so far during the season and wishing him a good summer.

Following John's advice, Matt launched an email to the parents of his team.

*Parents:*

*On behalf of all the coaches, I want to thank you for entrusting your children to us. They are an awesome group of kids and we enjoy working with them. As parents, you make a tremendous investment of time and energy to get them to practice and the games, and your continued support is greatly appreciated by all of us, both players and coaches.*

*Clearly, we are off to a rough start, and there are many areas that need improvement...players, coaches and parents as well.*

*While we are all a bit frustrated, there has been quite a bit of negative talk (if not outright insults) coming from our stands. Please take a moment and consider how this lands on the kids, and how this reflects upon the entire Bearcats team.*

*I want to remind us these are 10-year-olds, playing the game to have fun and be part of a team. The Bearcats are trying hard and we owe it to them to encourage them, not humiliate them when they're down.*

*So here's the new set of Parent expectations for all of us:*

- *We act with dignity.*
- *We maintain our perspective.*
- *We encourage all players on both teams.*
- *We use positive talk, cheer and encouragement only.*
- *Only the Head Coach addresses the officials or other teams' parents/coaches.*
- *Participate—get involved and be part of the solution, not part of the problem.*

*And finally, I welcome your feedback at any time.*

*Any issues need to be brought directly to me and we will meet face to face to discuss and resolve them, not over email. We can meet over a cup of coffee at the Full o' Beans coffee shop on Main Street. This way, your issues will receive the appropriate time and attention, without interruption. You can call, text or email me to set up a meeting.*

*Remember, this isn't about us, it's about the kids. They are why we do this.*

*Thanks again for your support, and all you're doing to help us have a successful season for the Bearcats.*

*Matt*

*P.S. Seriously...we have a couple of openings on the coaching staff and could use some help. If you're willing to devote some time to help our kids, let's talk about how you can be part of it.*

Matt read the message several times. What he really wanted to say was, "Act like grown-ups! Think about what your actions are teaching your kids!"

He finally hit send.

He felt certain his email would tick off the very parents it was intended to reach. It might make things worse. Although it was hard to imagine how.

### Coach's Rule #3

*Define clear expectations for players, coaches and parents; otherwise, a team's culture develops by default.*

# CHAPTER 4:
# STAFFING UP

Matt showed up at John's bright and early Monday morning. Two of his newer workers, Nick and L.J., were right behind him in Nick's truck.

Nick also worked part-time as one of the town's firefighters, and L.J. was a student in the HVAC program at the nearby community college. Both were short on experience but long on willingness to learn and work hard. John's project wasn't complicated and would be a great place for them to gain some experience while Matt figured out whether he could trust their judgment and their abilities. Matt planned to stick close during the process and use the project as an opportunity to teach them and give them plenty of one-on-one feedback.

After greeting John and filling him in on how the project would proceed, Matt walked Nick and L.J. through the project. Sipping his morning coffee, John listened from a chair on the back deck, while the dog who rarely left John's side sniffed around the back yard and rolled around a bit in the cool, early-spring grass near the edge of the woods.

"So where do we start?" Nick asked after some of the details had been covered.

"Where would you start?" Matt asked, feeling instinctively this was a teaching moment for his young crew.

"Well, I'd get rid of this ramp," Nick replied, taking a swallow of his own take-out coffee. "That's gonna be easy, so we can get it out of the way."

"I can see how that sounds like a good place to start," Matt said, nodding. "Here's another way to look at it. This ramp could make it easier for us to haul stuff in and out of the house. Once we take out the ramp, we'll have eight steps to go up and down to haul out the old shower stall and the kitchen island, not to mention bringing in the materials for the new island. And the new tub is going to be a bear. With the ramp, we can use a dolly. So what if we left the ramp for last?"

Nick grinned and nodded. "Hey, I'm all for making it easier."

Matt liked the easy way Nick followed his lead. "So let's start at the farthest point from the door—the bathroom—so we're not hauling stuff back and forth across our new kitchen when it's done."

"But doesn't it make things easier, too, if we rip out everything in the kitchen and the bathroom first, then start installing new stuff?" L.J. asked.

Matt nodded. "You're absolutely right. And I like the fact you're thinking about ways to be more efficient—keep thinking that way. Doing it that way would definitely be easier for us. But it would be miserable for customers. Their house in chaos—their lives disrupted—the whole time. John over there wouldn't be able to get his morning shower or his morning coffee without some hassle until we're done. Some decisions are about making it easier to do our jobs. My personal belief is it works better in the long haul to make some things easier for the customer, too."

Nick and L.J. nodded.

They worked steadily through the morning, first covering everything in the adjoining bedroom in drop cloths to minimize dust, then removing the old shower stall and taking it out to Matt's truck, to be carried away to a second-hand store that benefited a local charity. By lunch, old tile also had been ripped out. In the afternoon, they could begin prepping the space for installing the new tub, which Nick and L.J. would pick up while they were out getting lunch.

Matt had planned to grab his own lunch while on the way to another job site, but when John offered him a sandwich, he decided to stay. He liked the old man. Knowing a bit about what John had been through made Matt eager to be as kind as possible.

They sat on the deck overlooking the back yard. Behind the lot, Matt knew, was a large expanse of hilly woods the college used as a cross-country track. He had run and walked on the cleared eight-mile path many times over the years. It felt good to get in some exercise surrounded by nature, in an area quiet and isolated from noise and development. In the early mornings, Matt had often seen families of deer leaping across the path and rabbits scurrying for cover.

"I like the way you talk to your crew," John said as they chowed down. "Keeping it simple without talking down to them."

"They're good guys. I like working with young people." Matt grabbed some of the chips John had set out and smiled. "I used to think I was good at it, until I started coaching the Bearcats."

John laughed softly. "Well, coaching kids is a whole other ball game. Literally. And, frankly, a lot of your kids have never played before. That makes it tough. But is also creates a great opportunity since you're not really breaking any old bad habits. They don't have any yet!"

John turned a bit more serious. "So how is your people strategy coming along?"

This happened a lot, Matt decided. What seemed like casual conversation with John seemed to turn into more. In fact, John seemed to be doing the same thing he'd just done with Nick and L.J.—asking a few questions to get them thinking about their own assumptions. What assumptions did he have about coaching his team, Matt wondered, and how were those assumptions getting in his way? Matt decided to answer John's questions with a question of his own.

"So would you tell me about your coaching, John?"

"Oh sure. It was a long time ago, when my boy was a kid."

"Baseball?"

"Yes. Baseball was always my game of choice."

"So you played, as well?"

John shrugged and swallowed a bite of his sandwich. "High school. Not good enough for college."

"But good enough to coach," Matt countered.

"Well, I learned. It was rocky those first years. I had to learn the hard way there's a difference between *coaching* and *instructing.*"

"That's an interesting distinction," Matt said.

John studied him for a minute. "Instruction is about teaching game skills. Coaching is about revealing life skills. At least, that's how I came to look at it. The way you were doing with your crew this morning."

"What do you mean?"

"When you asked their opinion and listened and respected their input, then put it to them in a different light—that was coaching. That was giving them a new way of looking at the situation." John refilled their glasses of iced tea from a brightly-colored pitcher. "Now, if you'd been showing them the best way to remove the tile, that would have been instruction. Instead, you were teaching them how to think about their work. That's gonna stick with them. And it's going to be a lot more valuable than just how to rip out old tile and slap down new."

"I see what you're saying," Matt said. *"So I have to give the kids on the team both coaching and instruction?"*

"That's right Matt. The kids, parents, and other coaches." John affirmed. "To keep it straight in my head, I always considered the people strategy to be an important aspect of coaching, and separate from instruction. A good people strategy sets the team up for success on multiple levels, establishes a culture, sets expectations, and gets everybody on the same page."

Matt listened intently.

"And, if your actions are consistent with your people strategy, it builds trust in all of the relationships. It's really worth the effort on the front end." John smiled faintly. "Back in the day when I was in your shoes, I figured out I was a better coach than I was an instructor. It just wasn't in my skill set to know how to teach a kid to hit the ball better or make it around the bases quicker. I found some guys who had what it took to instruct, so I could focus on the people aspect. I considered finding good instruction for the kids an important part of my job as the coach."

"And what did it take to be a good instructor?"

"Oh, about ten thousand hours."

"What?"

John chuckled. "It takes a lot of hands-on experience to really sharpen a skill—some studies say it takes about ten thousand hours to become an expert. You have many times that in your profession, Matt. Over time, I figured out the longer somebody had been part of the game, the more he knew. Guys who played in high school were way better instructors than the ones who hadn't. And guys who played in college were even better instructors than the ones who only played in high school."

"That makes sense," Matt said. "But what's left to coach if somebody else is teaching the kids how to bat and throw and pitch and catch?"

John's smile got bigger, and Matt had the distinct impression he'd just missed the coaching point. "Oh, I don't know. Did you send out a message to the parents the other night and set some expectations going forward?"

Matt nodded his head he did.

"So then who is left?" asked John.

There he was with the questions again.

"Well I guess that leaves the Bearcat players and coaches, and maybe the players, parents and coaches on the other teams. And oh yeah, the officials."

John asked, "Ok then, what kinds of important things should you be talking about with your players? And what types of commitments are you looking for from your coaches to support and reinforce those important things?"

Matt thought about it while he took a long swallow from his tea. "How to work together. How to respect one another. How to support others on the team."

"There you go. That's a start."

"What kind of effort is expected. How to be dependable and consistent."

"Ah you mean trust. That's a big one," John said. "

"Trust?" Matt waited. He was learning it was well worth waiting to see what the older man had to say.

"You have any other jobs going on right now, Matt?"

"Sure. We're framing up a garage in the next town, and we're finishing out a bonus room for a professor here in town."

"But you're not there. You've been here all morning. Who's running those shows for you?"

"I have a couple of crew chiefs."

"And these guys, Nick and L.J., they're new?"

56

"That's right."

"So your crew chiefs…how'd they get to be the ones who take the lead when you're not around?"

"Well, they have experience. They've learned how I want things done. And…they are dependable."

"Dependable. What makes them dependable?"

"I know I can count on them," Matt said. "They show up when they're supposed to, do the work up to certain standards. And they're predictable. They deliver consistently, even when I'm not there."

"So over time, you have learned to trust them."

Matt nodded. "Yeah."

"I'll bet they trust you, too. They know you're going to be fair, pay them on time, make sure they have the materials and the extra hands and the other conditions they need to do their work well.

"I hope so."

"So even if one of you has an off day, if something happens you can't control or even if you make a mistake, there's enough trust between all of you to maintain and hopefully grow the relationships."

Matt thought about the defeat on the faces of the kids after their third loss. He wondered how much trust was lost when a team kept losing. Yet losing was part of the game; even the best teams lost.

"And trust —it's important to a coach?"

"Not just important—it's essential. They have to trust you, and you have to trust them," John said. "That's why you had to let that third-base coach know what's what the other night. He's destroying his trust with not only that kid, but all the kids and parents that witnessed it. When that happens, the kids don't feel safe."

"Safe?"

"Sure. You think it's easy for a kid to go out on the field in front of everybody and risk messing up? Risk losing?"

"But everybody loses," Matt said.

John nodded. "Sports is a great place to learn how to fail."

Matt shook his head. His conversations with John always seemed to turn his thinking upside down. "Wait. What do you mean? I thought a coach's job is to teach kids how to win."

John shrugged. "Winning will come after you put certain things in place—a healthy culture, clear expectations, solid instruction, and good old fashioned hard work. But you undermine all of it if the kids can't trust you to treat them fairly and consistently when they fail...lose...or otherwise mess up. Failure is a part of life. It is how you respond to your failures that eventually leads to achieving success, and perhaps in your case, a few extra wins." He paused, as if to make sure Matt understood the distinction he was making.

Matt frowned. "How to fail?"

"One of the best things about kids' sports is it gives them a chance to accept failure as a part of life, to learn how to get over the failures fast and move on, over and over again."

"So I need to coach them on how to fail without thinking it means *they* are a failure."

"Ah! That's a great way to put it. Coach the behavior, coach the result, but for goodness sake, don't condemn the kid. That would be missing the whole point of youth athletics!"

"Yeah," Matt said, smiling as he realized John had carefully and intentionally led him to something really significant. "And not just kids, parents and coaches, too."

John wadded up his paper napkin and dropped it onto his plate. "Baseball is great for teaching us how to fail, isn't it? It's a game of failure—we are out more than we are safe. Every inning has no less than three failed at bats. Kind of like life."

"And baseball's a pretty safe place for a kid to learn that," Matt said, making sure he could articulate all the key ideas John had led him to during their lunch.

"It can be. If you have a coach with the right approach."

*A big if,* Matt thought.

"Baseball is an equal opportunity game; you can learn just as much from losing as you can from winning, and sometimes more."

The sleeping dog drowsed awake, ambled over to the table and nudged John's knee. John tore off a bite of the turkey from the remains of his sandwich and held it out for Buster.

"As I recall," John said, "coaching kids can feel like a fairly thankless job. Impossible to please everybody."

"Nothing's changed about that, I'm afraid. And just when you think it can't get any worse, I lost two of my assistant coaches after the last game. The one who was yelling at the kid on third base—I pretty much drove him out the door. The other one was his buddy, and he'd resigned by the time I got home to my email."

"Probably not much of a loss," John said. "Trust is part of leadership. If they don't understand how their actions impact a kid's trust, they're no leaders. These volunteer positions call for leadership and if the coaches aren't sensitive to that they don't belong on the staff."

"I suppose. But I'm starting to feel like I'm about to drown out there." Matt pushed back from the table and propped his foot on his knee. "Say, you really seem to know your stuff. How about reviving your career as a coach? I could sure use the help."

"Oh, no, I don't think so. I'm a little past my peak for coaching. But, say, I did talk to one of the dads last night— Charlie was his name. Zack's dad. Seemed pretty sharp. You oughta talk to him."

It was a mark of how much Matt liked and respected John that he made up his mind right then to get in touch with this guy Charlie as soon as he could. If John thought he seemed sharp, he probably was. And Zack was one of the few players on the team who seemed to have a clue what he was doing out there.

### 

Shorthanded at the next practice, Matt suggested Will focus on working with half the team on fielding while Matt focused on batting with the other half. After thirty minutes, they swapped groups.

After that, Will worked on drills to improve their base running. While that was going on, Matt took each kid aside for a few minutes to get acquainted. He asked them what they liked about baseball, what they wanted to be doing on the field and a little bit about their families. He asked them what other sports they played, and for how long. Matt took notes. By the time practice was winding down, Matt was beginning to get a sense of the interest level, the maturity level, and the true athletic experience of each kid on the team, which was a start.

Jackson, the lead-off hitter, had been through a growth spurt and hadn't yet learned how to work with his suddenly longer arms and legs. He could play infield or outfield and, after talking with him, Matt put him on the list as a possible pitcher. He had two older brothers who had been teaching him the game for years.

Zack was next in the batting order. Another solid player, he could play any infield position, and his dimensions and nifty glove made him a strong candidate for first base. He was just a reliable kid—a real leader in the making. A strong, likeable kid with good balance and decent speed, Zack hit and ran well. His dad was Charlie, the guy John mentioned I should talk with.

Brady was next. A freckled redhead, Brady was a little bit of a cut-up, but seemed like a dependable kid. Matt decided to suggest him as another pitcher for the team. He also was a decent fielder. He didn't talk much about his family, even when encouraged.

Jermaine, Ethan and Hunter were next in the line-up and all had decent athletic ability. They hung out together and all three were trouble, in different ways.

Jermaine, an African American with a dimpled smile and a sparkle in his eyes, was a happy-go-lucky kid who could be a player if he decided to focus. He'd been catching and batting clean-up. He was not a great catcher, but Matt wasn't sure he had a better option.

Ethan, a tall blond boy whose family had moved from California earlier in the year, was an attention-seeker with a tendency to bully. He played short stop and centerfield. He wanted to pitch, so Matt added him to his list of options as a pitcher. Matt's main reservation about Ethan was that he seemed to be a ring-leader among those who tended to goof off, and he didn't seem to have much respect for the team.

Hunter, well he was just Hunter. A sometime brooding kid with dark-hair, dark-eyes and slight. Sometimes Matt could see Hunter playing anywhere, and other times he could see him playing nowhere, depending on whatever attitude Hunter brought with him that day. He also avoided answering any questions about his family or his personal life.

Then there was Taylor, arguably their best pitcher, and one of only three girls in the entire league. Matt was beginning to think she was a natural athlete, maybe better than anyone except Zack. She was a solid pitcher, hard to rattle, with a lot of control for a kid her age. As a hitter, she could be counted on to make contact with the ball. And she could run pretty darn fast—faster than most of the other kids on the team.

These kids were the backbone of his team. Contrary to his initial impression, Matt was starting to believe many of these kids had potential. However, they needed instruction and better coaching too—now that Matt was beginning to understand the difference.

Matt had to figure out how to turn that potential into some kind of positive outcome for his team.

Maybe the key was John's third bit of implied advice—he needed to find some other parents who could give instruction in the skills Matt didn't have. A qualified coaching staff could make all the difference.

The rest of the Bearcats didn't offer much. Luke was a sweet kid and he was beginning to get to Matt, the way he always looked sort of lost and hopeful at the same time. Luke wanted it really badly, but he seemed to be afraid of the ball and he had a tendency to daydream. He actually had a decent arm and, if he could engage, Luke probably could handle third base.

Gabe and Eli were really small for their ages, but Gabe was fast and showed some promise as a hitter—which could be a plus, given he had such a small strike zone—and Eli...well, Eli was a sweet kid. Who knows, maybe he could learn to bunt or something. Their moms showed up for games more than their dads, and Matt wondered if the boys came from broken homes.

Then there was Mason—the kid who held himself like he'd been playing the game forever, but would not engage with the ball in any way whatsoever. Matt supposed the boy might have some developmental challenges, but he didn't know enough to figure out what the situation might be or how to handle it. He made a mental note to talk to Mason's parents to gain some insights into the boy. He owed it to the kid, and to the team, to find a way to coach Mason.

*And good luck with that,* he thought as he watched Mason remain motionless through five practice pitches.

The best thing about this night's practice turned out to be Luke's mother, Sarah Kate.

Matt had observed, out of the corner of his eye, as she took photos during the practice and worked the crowd, talking to the other parents. They seemed to like her. So after they finished up a practice that didn't feel much more effective than the previous practice, Matt was happy when Sarah Kate approached him instead of one of the grousers and complainers.

"I wanted to thank you for your email after the last game, Matt. That was a really good message."

Up close, he could see the resemblance to Luke—right down to the sad look in her eyes. But she smiled, just the way she had smiled at the other parents she interacted with, and seemed unwilling to give in to that sadness. Matt tried not to think about what it would be like to lose Traci, the way Sarah Kate had lost her husband. Matt couldn't imagine getting up and facing the day without Traci.

"Thanks, Sarah Kate. I'm not sure everybody agrees with you."

She laughed softly. "Well, parents can forget that, for kids, having fun can be just as important as winning. Listen, I thought about what you said about helping out and I was wondering how you'd feel if I set up a team page on Facebook. You know, just a place where we could post pictures and reminders about practice times and things like that. I'm not trying to be pushy or anything, but I like taking pictures and I stay in touch with my sisters and my girlfriends from college on Facebook, so I thought, well, it couldn't hurt. Team spirit-wise, I mean."

"I think that would be great. I wouldn't have time to do much with it myself, of course."

"No, of course not. I'd be happy to be the page administrator. I'd add you as an administrator, too, naturally. But I like Facebook and sort of being the connector, if you know what I mean."

"Thanks, Sarah Kate. I really appreciate you for stepping up."

"Great! I'll set it up tonight." She turned to leave, then paused and turned back to him. "Oh. Say, about Mason…"

"Yeah?"

"He's a little different, you know?"

Matt shook his head and smiled faintly. "I noticed."

"I mean, he's in my class at school. And he's…maybe it's not my place to say this, but he's on the spectrum, in case it helps to know that."

"On the spectrum?"

"The autism spectrum. Asperger's Syndrome. He's very high-functioning compared to some children on the spectrum. And really smart. Just different, especially in how he interacts with people. And he can just zero in on something and be really brilliant about it. His mom says he's crazy about baseball." She paused and seemed to see in Matt's face he didn't quite know what to do with this information now that he had it. "Sometimes it helps to know what you're dealing with."

And what, Matt wondered, was he dealing with? He knew nothing about autism or Asperger's. "Sure. Thanks again. That's good to know."

As he sat down in front of his computer later that night and researched autism and Asperger's Syndrome, Matt thought, *Shouldn't it be easier than this?* He saw some indicators that certainly helped him understand Mason—his tendency to hyper-focus and filter out distractions or things he wasn't interested in, for example. And Sarah Kate was right—kids with Asperger's often were extremely bright.

Although Matt knew he didn't have what it took to help a kid like Mason, it made him even more committed to doing what he could. If the boy wanted to be on the baseball team, Matt wanted to figure out how to make it a great experience for him.

### 

Matt looked down at the faces that were finally becoming familiar to him and wondered what a good coach would say to them. Here they were, about to head into their fourth game, with three losses and no wins under their belt. What could he say to fire them up? Should he tell them this was their time, and they had to win this one?

Most important, should he give them hope by telling them the team they were about to play had the same losing record they did?

And if he told them this, how much worse would a loss feel?

He took a deep breath and let it out slowly. "Okay, listen up, Bearcats! You've worked hard this week. And we're going to keep working hard today! Right?"

A few kids shuffled their feet, a couple muttered a response, one rolled his eyes. Luke, Zack and Taylor, responded with a hopeful, "Right!"

"That's right," Matt said. "You bet we are! The guys in that dugout over there are no better than we are. They are a bunch of ten year olds just like us."

He hoped that was true. He saw Luke nodding, with a hopeful smile on his face, and was doubly hopeful it was true.

"So today, we're just going to focus on a few things. First, we need to pay attention to what is going on in the game. Before the ball is hit to you, try to figure out where you throw the ball if you get it. Be sure to consider if there are baserunners, ok?"

Matt paused to let the effect of his "pay attention" speech sink in.

"Second, let's do our best today. Sometimes your best is good enough to win the game, and sometimes it's not. But we can control how hard we try, so let's just focus on that."

Again, Matt paused to see if he could detect a pulse. Eyes blinked.

"And third, for goodness sake, let's have fun. This is a game after all."

Now that got a response, as half the kids shifted their feet, popped their fist in their gloves, and smiled. Fun was apparently a concept ten year olds could understand.

Matt repeated the three mantras of "pay attention", "do your best" and "have fun" a couple more times, and feeling inspired, moved onto a few finer points they had worked on in practice.

"Remember we want every fly ball to be an out." Matt looked around and wondered if any of the kids were really listening at all. "Let's remember that, Bearcats. Fly balls are what?"

The kids looked around, waiting for someone else to speak.

Zack said, "Outs!"

"Thanks, Zack. Let's hear it from the rest of you. Fly balls are…?"

"Outs!" came the slightly less tentative response from the team.

It wasn't a wildly enthusiastic chorus, but it felt like progress.

"Okay! Let's hit the field!" Matt urged.

And with that final bit of inspiration, the Bearcats straggled out to take the field.

In the top of the first inning, Taylor managed to retire the side singlehandedly with three quick strike-outs. Matt started to feel hopeful. Apparently, in the dugout, the rest of the team did, too, as an excited murmur emanated from that general direction. In the bottom of the first, Jackson made it to first base on a walk. Then Zack hit a shot to right which moved Jackson over to third. The Bearcats had a player in scoring position in the first inning and no outs! Then Brady struck out. Jermaine popped straight up to the catcher.

Jackson was not paying attention on third and got doubled off by the catcher on Jermaine's pop up.

Inning over.

*So much for momentum,* Matt thought.

"Good effort," Will called when they huddled in front of the dugout before taking their positions.

"Remember, Bearcats," Matt said. "Fly balls are outs."

Zack looked at him and nodded. The other players trudged out to the field without acknowledging him.

The next several innings were a contest to see which team could bungle things the most. By the end of the fifth, no one had scored. In the top of the sixth, Mason was leading off. Matt told himself that was okay—even after Mason earned his obligatory out, the top of the lineup would be up with only one out.

True to form, Mason stood perfectly still through a strike and two balls. Matt began to wonder if Mason would be as reluctant to run as he was to bat. What if he got a walk and just stood there?

*Don't borrow trouble,* Matt reminded himself. *Two balls do not make a walk.*

The third throw was a perfect strike, right across the plate. Mason maintained his stance.

Matt wanted to laugh when he realized Mason's reaction seemed to have completely undone the young pitcher, who couldn't figure out what was going on. The fourth throw was another wild ball. A player on base could've advanced a base. They were one pitch away from a walk.

Wishing bad luck on a kid just seemed wrong, but Matt had to admit he hoped the young pitcher for the other team did not get his act together.

The final throw was inside. Mason didn't flinch. The ump signaled a walk. The Bearcats' dugout and the stands went wild.

Mason stood there, bat dangling at his side.

"Come on, Mason!" Matt said under his breath, hoping and praying the boy didn't humiliate himself by freezing up. "Run to first. Please, kid, run to first."

After a couple of seconds to process what was happening, Mason ran with a long, steady stride to first base.

Matt went over to high-five Mason, who kept his eyes down but did manage to slap hands with his coach. There might've been the faintest of smiles on his face.

"Okay, Mason. Jackson's up. You know what to do when he hits the ball, right?"

"Yeah." Mason thought about it for a second. "Run."

"That's right, buddy. Run! Run fast."

That's just what he did, too, when Jackson hit a looping line drive to right-center field. Mason kicked into gear and made it all the way to third base, where Will signaled him to stay.

Jackson made it to second for a double. Matt was almost in shock. This might be the first time they'd managed to get two runners in scoring position so far this season. He realized his heart was pounding with excitement. And the roar from the Bearcats' bleachers sounded World-Series caliber in his ears.

Uncharacteristically, Zack struck out. Brady was up. Matt caught Will's attention on the third base line and nodded toward Mason, a signal to remind Mason to run if Brady managed a hit.

"Come on, Brady," he called out. "Base hit. That's all we need. A base hit."

Behind him, however, he could hear a couple of parents urging Brady to unleash for the fence—which was exactly why he had struck out every time so far today.

Brady dug in and waited for the ball. It looked a little high to Matt, up in his eyes, but Brady gave it the Babe Ruth treatment and spun halfway around, never coming close to the ball. The second pitch was another strike and Matt resigned himself to the very real possibility of losing this opportunity to score. There was every chance they would lose to the other worst team in the league.

He reminded himself it was only a game.

Then he heard the crack of the ball against the aluminum bat, and Brady was running in his direction.

Matt looked at third. Mason was already heading in, running with surprising speed, and Jackson was about ready to round third base.

Everyone was on their feet, shouting and cheering.

The Bearcats had two runs! On a rally started by a kid who hadn't swung the bat all season!

### 

The rest of the game was anti-climactic. The rally was halted when Jermaine struck out. With the score at 2-0, Bearcats, there was no more action to speak of. But the Bearcats finally had something in the win column. And nobody made mention of the fact the team they'd beaten was another cellar-dweller.

Following an exuberant pep talk after the game, everyone packed up and headed off. Matt was happy to note John had been on hand for the win and gave him a wave. When he did, John pointed at the man sitting next to him—Zack's dad, Charlie, Matt supposed. The guy John had mentioned earlier in the week. Matt nodded to acknowledge John's signal and headed in the direction of Charlie, who was bumping knuckles with Zack.

"Congratulations on the win, Zack," Matt said as he walked up.

"Thanks, Coach. Sorry I struck out."

Matt tugged on the bill of Zack's ball cap. "It happens to the best of us, buddy. You always do your share."

He extended his hand to Charlie. "I'm Matt. I believe you're Charlie."

"That's right." They shook hands.

"I hear you've been around the game a while," Matt said, deciding to test John's ten thousand hour theory.

"I played in high school and a couple of years in college," Charlie said. "I wasn't a star player or anything, but I've hung around a lot of dugouts."

*Bingo!* Matt did a mental fist-pump. "I was wondering if I could talk to you about helping out a little with the team."

"Well, I'm out of town with my job a lot. But—"

"Congratulations, Matt!" It was Sarah Kate, with Luke at her side. Luke was beaming as broadly as if the winning run had been his.

"Thanks, Sarah Kate." He looked at the two of them and quickly made up his mind. "Listen, I need help. And I think you two would be terrific assets for the team. Sarah Kate, I'd like you to be the team coordinator. And I was just about to make Charlie here an offer he can't refuse."

Charlie laughed. "Like I said, I'm gone a lot, but I'd be glad to help however I can."

Sarah Kate looked down at Luke, then back at Matt with conviction. "I'm not sure what the team coordinator does, but if you think I can help, I'll give it my best shot."

By the time Matt made it to his truck, the three of them had spoken with Will and arranged a meeting for the following night to make a plan for the rest of the season. And as he cranked the engine, a text message came through from one of the other parents: *Thanks for helping our boys. Don't know much about ball, but I used to coach tennis. If I can help, let me know. – B.J.*

It wasn't much of a win, but it was enough, apparently, to generate some enthusiasm, Matt told himself as he headed for home. He had his coaching staff, the people who were going to help him be a coach after all. He was sure of it.

## Coach's Rule #4

*Build a team of volunteers who have skills that complement yours, who share your passion and enthusiasm, and who align with your vision for the team.*

# CHAPTER 5:
# RESTART

Matt couldn't wait to tell John about his new coaches when he showed up on the job the next morning.

A team of assistant coaches felt like a chance for a major overhaul, a complete shift at mid-season. Maybe that sounded a little crazy. Even Traci had said it was sort of like waking up one morning and finding out his business had three new crew chiefs and only one old hand.

"How can you be sure they aren't all going to have their own ideas about how to do things?" she had asked, and he'd realized he wasn't sure at all. After all, they probably hadn't signed on because they thought he was doing such a terrific job. His best hope, Matt decided, was they will come with ideas, commitment and flexibility.

The chance to set things right after such a lousy start was exhilarating, but it also was a little intimidating. After all, the first half of the season had pretty much been a disaster; he didn't want to blow this chance to turn things around.

*Maybe,* he thought, walking around to the back deck where John typically was enjoying his coffee with the morning newspaper when Matt arrived, *John will be good for a little advice about how to handle things.*

"Congratulations on the win," John said as Matt rounded the corner.

Buster thumped his tail to acknowledge Matt's arrival and settled his head back onto his paws to continue his nap.

"Thanks," Matt said, feeling a little sheepish the game was even considered a win. "I'm afraid that was more a case of 'both teams can't lose' than one team actually being better than the other."

John chuckled. "The win's in your column. A win's a win, even an ugly win. There's coffee in the kitchen. Help yourself."

"Thanks."

Matt went into the kitchen and poured himself a cup. This had become his ritual for starting the day. He came by John's first thing, had a cup of coffee and a little conversation with John, made sure his young crew showed up and knew what to do with themselves the rest of the day, checked on progress from the day before, then headed for the other jobs which were underway.

Before he went back outside, Matt stuck his head in the bathroom. Nick had texted him the afternoon before the bathroom was completed, so Matt checked it out thoroughly. The new tile looked great, the walls had been sanded down and freshly painted, and L.J. had cleaned up the caulk and the dust. The room looked good and ready for use.

"Looks like we're ready to turn your kitchen into a war zone," he said as he walked back out.

"Yep. The boys did a nice job on the bathroom."

"Good. Just let me know if you see anything that needs attention. Anything at all."

"I will."

Matt sat at the table and sipped his coffee.

"Guess that means you'll be bringing coffee tomorrow morning," John said. "Unless you like sawdust in your java."

Matt chuckled. "I'll bring the coffee."

"So how'd it go with Charlie? You get a chance to talk to him?"

"Yeah, I did. He's going to help out. And Sarah Kate—that's Luke's mom—"

"The friendly little lady with the camera?" asked John.

"That's the one. She's going to be the team coordinator. And another guy who used to coach tennis stepped up and offered to help."

"Congratulations, Matt. Sounds like you have a completely overhauled coaching staff."

"True. It's a great opportunity, isn't it?"

"Is that a little apprehension I hear in your voice?"

"Maybe. I mean, it's great, unless I can't capitalize on it." He looked over at John and grinned wryly. "Unless I screw this up, too."

"Bah! You didn't screw up. You stepped into the middle of a mess."

"Yeah, maybe. But if I'd been sharper... more experienced... I might've cleaned up the mess a little better than I did—and a little faster."

"Well, you have a chance now. That's what counts. It's like a restart."

Matt took a big swallow of coffee. "Traci asked me last night how I could be sure the three of them—even Will, for all I know—won't come in with their own ideas about what we ought to be doing. I mean, it's not necessarily a bad thing for them to have some ideas, unless the five of us just end up fighting over how to salvage the season. That could be a disaster."

"It's up to you not to let that happen."

"Me? How do I do that?"

"You're the coach." John looked him squarely in the eye. "Aren't you?"

"Yes."

"So as the head coach, it is your job to erect the framework you and your other coaches can build upon to deliver a successful season. This framework consists of two distinct strategies; the people strategy, which I have already mentioned, and your game strategy, which we can discuss later."

Matt listened on.

"Now here's a key point. Ready? It takes both a *people strategy* and a *game strategy* to have a special season for the kids. And both strategies can provide your team with advantages which will help you win games. Let's talk about finishing your people strategy. You have already sent out the Parent expectations. So that leaves two groups to address; the players and the coaches."

"That's right," acknowledge Matt.

"By the end of my coaching career, I learned to start each season by creating three sets of mantra statements to set the tone, one for each group. I called them player rules, parent expectations, and coaching commitments."

Matt was scribbling some notes. "Player rules. Parent expectations. Coaching commitments. Got it. I already have an idea as to what those might be."

John cleared his throat and went on. "Now once you have your people strategy in place, you and your coaches will need to build your game strategy together."

Matt cocked his head to the side. "What's the game strategy entail?"

Great question, replied John. "The game strategy is about the instruction. It's about developing the individual players and their knowledge of the game, and relevant skills, techniques and fundamentals. To instruct them properly, you need to assess them to know what you have, and then assign them one or two positions that are a good fit, taking into consideration where to position individual players to arrive at the best overall team."

John continued, "Then, you build practice routines that are efficient and effective for developing the fundamentals. Pull it all together by teaching situational strategies, like bunt defense, then executing a game plan."

"These are the nuts and bolts of a winning team, hopefully taught by people that know what they are doing, and are doing it for the right reasons."

This was a light bulb moment for Matt. "I get it, the people strategy is the coaching piece, and the game strategy is the instruction piece. I can see the distinction clearly now."

"Great." Said John.

"But Charlie, B.J., Will and Sarah Kate aren't kids. Maybe they'll have different or even better ideas than I have."

John chuckled. "Doesn't a great boss always hope his people will have better ideas?" He leaned across the table. "Go in first with your ideas. Talk about your desired outcomes, what you think will be important for the Bearcats this season and for each player. Ask them what they think matters the most, and build it all into a framework that defines the program and works towards the outcomes you all agree with. Then ask 'em to commit and help you take the team there. But always remember—you're the coach. Step up and coach. You gotta lead it."

### 

All afternoon, as he drove from job to job, Matt thought about what John had said.

*You're the coach. Aren't you?*

*You're the coach. Step up and coach. And that means everyone.*

Matt thought about how John kept comparing his interactions with his work crew to his responsibilities as a coach. It was an intriguing idea and halfway through the afternoon he realized almost without thinking about it, he had been making mental notes about the way he handled himself as the boss.

On the job, he spoke with confidence. He listened with an open mind. He encouraged others to think. He weighed options and encouraged discussion. And he took full responsibility for the ultimate decisions and the outcomes. Maybe that was the basic action plan for a head coach, too.

By the end of the afternoon, he was excited about the seed John had planted and wanted to talk more about it. So, after checking with Traci, he made plans to accompany John and Buster on their evening walk after dinner.

The afternoons were getting longer and there was still plenty of daylight when Matt, John and Buster set off from John's house at six o'clock. They walked up the quiet street, where John waved at people setting out summer flowers or walking their own dogs. He even seemed to know all the children riding their bikes or dragging basketball goals out of garages and into cul-de-sacs. Matt suddenly had a greater appreciation for his new friend, who apparently had become the community grandfather in the short time he'd been in Stonefield.

"So you've been thinking about this restart of yours," John said when they reached a long stretch of wide sidewalk which, ultimately, would end up on Main Street.

"I have. And I wondered if…well, if you'd be my coach." Matt sensed John's reaction and hastened to add, "I know. You don't want to coach. But I'm talking about being the coach's coach. Unofficially. Just until I get myself squared away."

"We could maybe do that," John said. "But my services don't come cheap. It's likely to cost you a lot of coffee."

Matt laughed. "I can swing that."

"So where do you want to start?"

"I jotted some ideas down today, while I was visiting my job sites," Matt said, pulling his phone out of his pocket and opening the notes app. "And I thought about how you said I should build the game strategy with the coaches. So I set up a meeting for tomorrow night, before our first practice together."

"Good thinking," John said.

"Yeah. I guess I need to sell my people strategy to them, and then we all work together to build the game strategy? Do I have that right?"

John nodded his head and laughed, and Matt found himself laughing along with him.

"I'm really not unsure of myself," Matt said. "Business owners can't afford to be and I've learned to be pretty confident. It's just…I don't want to mess this up any more than it's already messed up."

"You're wise to be thinking that way, Matt," responded John. "And I like how you're connecting this with how you conduct yourself as a boss. I've watched you interact with Nick and L.J., and you have the demeanor of a natural coach with them."

"Thanks. So how do I translate that into this situation with these new coaches? I mean, they're all volunteers. They don't have to take orders. I've already seen what can happen if you crack down on volunteers who don't like what you're telling them. So what do I do?"

They paused while Buster sniffed out the base of a large oak tree. "How do you start when you have a new project for your work crews?" John prompted.

"I'll bring everybody together, tell them what the client wants, ask for their ideas, then scope out the big picture. Tell them who's going to do what, that kind of thing."

"In other words, you start with a vision—the client's vision?" asked John.

Matt scratched his head, "Vision is kind of a big word for a construction project—or a kids' ball team. Isn't it?"

"Not for the client who has that vision," John said. "And not for the kids and the parents on that ball team. A vision is just a mental picture of what it's going to look like when you've accomplished what you set out to accomplish, isn't it?"

"Yes."

"In youth sports, it has to be easy to understand, remember and repeat. Wouldn't you say?"

Matt nodded. "Our vision for the Bearcats is where we end up, so it's our outcomes, and it should be simple and easy to understand and repeat, so it should be included in our people strategy, right?"

John added, "And you want everybody looking toward the same outcomes so everybody agrees and has the same expectations."

Matt tapped a note into his phone. "Then what's the vision for the Bearcats?"

John smiled at him. "Can't tell you that. You're the coach. The vision has to start with you. But here's a couple tips for you. First, your season vision has to be aligned tightly with your "why" you coach the team. Second, your season vision should include multiple levels of success, so if you don't win on the scoreboard, you can still have a positive experience for the kids, and something they can learn from, feel good about, and build upon after they leave your team and move onto their next one."

Matt sighed, "Ok. But...when it's a construction project, the vision comes from the client."

John nodded. "In a sense. But as the guy with the experience and the expertise, you have to translate what's in the client's head into a concrete vision—something that's actually attainable, and something which can be shared and easily understood by all. As the coach, what do your clients—the kids and their parents—want?"

"To win."

"Do they? Is that what you're charged with accomplishing? If you were sitting in the stands, and some other guy was coaching Maelee, would winning the game be the most important thing to you as a parent...or would you perhaps want something else for her, too?"

"Sure. Of course, I'd want more."

"Ok, like what?"

"Well, first of all I would want her to be treated well. I would want her to enjoy what she was doing, have fun, make friends, but also make progress learning skills. I suppose those could be skills related to that particular sport, or even life skills like competitiveness, courage, toughness, or just getting along with her teammates. Come to think of it, I would have a lot of expectations of Maelee's coaches other than just winning games.

John sat back and let that all sink on Matt, whose blank stare told John dots were connecting and Matt was getting the bigger picture.

"And of course, it also meant ...winning. Getting the highest score. "That matters too, right?" They were approaching a bench with a small water fountain at the edge of an expansive lawn; the homeowner had set out a dog bowl. John filled the bowl and set it down for Buster. Then, while Buster lapped up the fresh water, John sat on the bench and gestured for Matt to join him.

"When you walk with geezers, you have to take a break every now and then," he said.

Matt had asked a question, and he wondered if this little break wasn't just John's way of avoiding answering the question. He decided to wait him out.

It didn't work. By the time Buster had his fill of water and they stood to continue their walk, the question still hung in the air.

"If a client asks me to build a four thousand-square-foot house on three floors with a pool in the back, that's what I do," Matt said. "That's the client's vision."

"But is it a win?" John persisted. "If the lot is better suited to a nineteen hundred-square-foot bungalow, and there's only room in the back for a koi pond and the city won't approve plans for the four thousand-square-foot behemoth, isn't it your job to create strategies that actually are attainable?"

"So are you telling me I should tell the parents their kids can't win?"

"Of course not!" John gave him a long, hard look. "Is that what you believe? That these kids can't win?"

"No, but…" Matt sighed. "Well, maybe sometimes."

The shadow of a smile played across John's lined face. "Okay. Good to be honest here. Now are you willing to consider your job isn't just to win on the scoreboard, but is for your team to win on multiple levels—ways you define and communicate through your people and game strategies. Then, once you have aligned everyone—parents, players and coaches—on your program, you and your coaches will figure out how to get there. In my experience, if you follow this method, it will most certainly lead to wins on the scoreboard as well. This is how your team of individuals, with its particular strengths and weaknesses and skills, works together as a team to win games."

Matt felt some of his frustration begin to dissipate. Finally, something he could wrap his head around. "Yeah, I can see that."

"Good!" John clapped him on the shoulder.

Matt could see he was going to have to think harder about this for the Bearcats—and John wasn't going to tell him what it was supposed to be. As frustrating as it felt in the moment, Matt had a nagging feeling that John was demonstrating a good coaching technique by forcing him to think for himself.

*You're the coach. Step up and coach.*

"Okay. So when we start a new job, I paint the picture of this vision. Next, I ask my crew what they think. I get their ideas about how to move forward."

"How well does that work?" John asked.

Matt willed himself to set aside this riddle of a vision of winning for his team. "It works well enough. Sometimes the crew has good ideas. Sometimes discussing their ideas results in even better ideas. But in the end, the crew owns the plan because we've all talked it out."

"Does that sound like something that could work with your new coaching staff?"

Matt acknowledged it did.

They had reached Main Street. It was still busy as twilight began to fall, but the foot traffic was different now than it was during the middle of the day. During mid-day, it was full of college students and people purposefully carrying out errands—trips to the drug store or the post office or the library or the bank. Now, there were more people like Matt and John, taking leisurely walks with baby strollers and dogs, heading to or from one of the mom-and-pop restaurants or the ice cream parlor.

Matt's head was full, but he was aware, as they looped around Main Street and headed back toward John's neighborhood, he still had a lot of unanswered questions. Every conversation with John seemed to provoke more ideas he wanted to explore.

The mark of a good coach, he supposed.

They walked mostly in silence for a while, listening to the sounds of their little town—slow traffic, neighbors greeting neighbors, children playing, the birds and crickets that were starting their end-of-day communications.

As much as he enjoyed the quiet companionship, Matt was feeling the pressure of being about 24 hours away from meeting with his new assistants for the first time. "John, shouldn't I talk about this stuff when I meet with Charlie and the others?"

"You should."

Matt tapped more notes into his phone.

"That's part of your job as a coach," said John.

"You mean there's more?"

John nodded. "Once you and your coaches agree on your people and game strategies for the season, you have to communicate it consistently to players, parents, and each other. This is where the rubber meets the road if you're going to get traction. You have to be consistent, and everything you do should reinforce the things you agreed upon, and the 'why'—why you're coaching."

Matt saved the notes he'd made so far. "I have to tell you, John, this is starting to feel a little overwhelming and like a whole lot to do in short amount of time."

They paused at the corner of John's street. The old man put his hand on Matt's shoulder and looked him in the eye. "It'll feel better after you talk to your coaches."

"What if it doesn't?"

John smiled and walked on. "It will."

"See you in the morning, Matt. And don't forget the coffee."

## Coach's Rule #5

*Create a vision of success with multiple outcomes, some of which are totally within YOUR control, so the season can be a memorable success, even if the team's win column falls short. Ultimately, this is how you win on the scoreboard too.*

# CHAPTER 6:
# WHAT, WHEN AND HOW

Matt showed up on John's deck bright and early the next morning with the newspaper from the front yard and two cups of take-out coffee. John and Buster weren't out yet, so he sat in his usual spot and waited.

When John appeared at the back door, he smiled and picked up on the conversation from the night before. "Game strategies. Assess their ability, assign positions, develop skills and situational awareness, then execute a game plan. Assess, assign, develop, and execute...those are the basic steps."

Matt smiled and offered the coffee he'd brought for John. "That should be easy to remember. Okay."

John nodded his approval. "Good. That's a start. Now this is important. Every team is different, and so is every kid. After you make an initial assessment and assignment, be flexible and open minded. If necessary, make adjustments as you go. Some kids develop faster than others. Pay attention how they learn. You rarely get all of the assignments right the first time around."

Matt blinked.

"Here's another way to say it. Your initial assessment is critical because it creates your starting point or benchmark to measure progress against for each player and the team in general. After you know where you are starting, you and your coaches create a vision of an end point by asking yourselves "What is possible?" Then you and your coaches just have to make sure you build a plan to fill in the gap between the two."

"That makes a lot of sense," Matt continued. "Now what can you share about practice routines?"

"Practice is like your workshop, or assembly line. It has to develop the kids in a purposeful and efficient manner toward the vision. Establish your practice stations. Everybody—coaches, kids, even the parents—has to know what to do when they show up. Nothing's haphazard, nothing's by chance. It's all intentional and it all reinforces your agreed upon game strategy. And it has to address both individual player development, and also work on the situational stuff the team needs to execute successfully in games."

Matt said, nodding at John's smile. "Should I let the instruction guys figure out what practice looks like?"

"As long as there's a consistency to what they're doing and it makes sense to you. As long as their plan covers the fundamentals, let them take the lead. And if you do it right, you might find, after a while, the kids will be able to run the practice all by themselves. This by the way is another successful outcome of a special season."

Matt let it all begin to sink in. "And this is how we win? That's ... pretty simple. Are you sure?"

"That's only part of it." There was another one of John's long pauses. "In your construction business, you have a fair amount of competition, I suppose."

Matt nodded. "'Fraid so."

"Tell me this: What do you do to stand out from the crowd?"

Finally, something Matt felt confident talking about. He'd given a lot of thought to this over the half-dozen years he'd been in business. "I build the business on relationships. I listen to my clients, I pay attention to what's important to them. And I hire people who are able to listen and communicate well, because they're my eyes and ears in the field. I can't be on site every minute of every day."

"And that works for you?"

"I think it does. Most of my business comes from referrals. People seem to trust us."

"That's your advantage, Matt. That's *how* you win. Every other business out there has the same tools you have—hammers and screwdrivers and all the other stuff you have piled in those trucks of yours. But you've figured out how to give yourself an edge; you focus on relationships, and you do the small to medium-sized jobs better than anybody." John finished off his coffee. "Then you hire a few really good people and teach them how to do what you've learned. That's how you build a winning business—even when some of the big competitors bid against you. That's your edge."

John tapped a finger on the table top. "What kind of advantage can you give those kids of yours? And I'll give you a clue; it's not all athletic skills and baseball techniques, those are just part of it. Kids this age play best when they feel good about themselves, and you need to make it so. Figure all that out and build a program around it. That's your job,

Matt. Find a way they can all win, and work together to make it happen."

### 

The next evening, Matt looked around the table upstairs at the Full o' Beans coffee shop on Main Street and felt the full weight of the Bearcats' season shift off his shoulders.

Charlie, B.J., Will and Sarah Kate sat around the table with Matt, stirring their coffee and getting to know each other. For the first time in weeks, Matt felt optimistic.

"You have no idea how glad I am to see all of you tonight," he said after they chatted for a while. He was surprised at how deeply he meant it.

"Me, too," Will said. "At least if the other parents decide to run us out of town, we'll have some company."

Everyone laughed.

"We're off to a grim start, that's for sure," said B.J.

"Here's what I'm proposing," Matt said, having given a lot of thought to his conversations with John for the last couple of days. "I suggest we restart the season."

Four sets of eyes gave him a confused look.

"I know," Matt said. "We can't change the win-loss record. We're stuck with a 1-3 start. And thank goodness, finally we have something in the win column."

The other coaches nodded.

"But I think we can finish this season a lot different from the way we started out," Matt said. "I'm not saying we're going to win the league or anything. I'm just saying we can give these kids a season they can enjoy and be proud of."

The four people at the table began to glance at each other and nod.

"But we can only do that if the five of us agree on how to get from where we are now to where we want to be in another six weeks," Matt concluded. "And that's what I want us to talk about tonight. Ready?"

"Ready," Sarah Kate said and the others chimed in.

"Great! Now before we start, I want to ask you a question. When you were a kid, what made you love sports? What did you enjoy about it? Why'd you want to keep playing?"

They glanced around at each other. Charlie spoke first. "I didn't realize it at the time, but I just liked having a place where I fit in. We were all teammates, and friends."

A burly guy with the build of a linebacker, Charlie had earned a leadership position in the group after he told them about his own experience as a successful college athlete—a story he had related in a very humble way which immediately made him likable, as well as someone to follow.

B.J., who had already talked about playing tennis from an early age, said, "I wasn't a big kid and, honestly, I wasn't very good at academics." Will and Charlie chuckled and nodded, as if B.J. had struck a nerve. "So when I found tennis, it was felt good to have somebody finally telling me I could be good at something."

In his mid-thirties, B.J. still had the lean look of someone who could move like lightning across a tennis court. He was also blond, like his son Jackson.

"I felt like that, too," Sarah Kate said. "I didn't play sports, but I was in the marching band. I just loved hanging out with other kids who liked the same thing I did. And when we got to play for the football games…I don't know…it just felt great to be making a contribution while doing something we could get some positive attention for." She looked down, her cheeks growing pink. "I was kind of awkward, and awkward adolescents don't get a lot of positive attention. So I think I really feel for some of our kids who aren't necessarily…you know…the cool kids."

Matt looked at Will, who seemed startled by Sarah Kate's admission.

"Wow," Will said.

"Yes, being part of something, but it was more than that." Sarah started to speak softly as her hand moved to the small gold cross hanging loosely around from her neck on a thin chain. "Serving in the band was consistent with what my father always said about having a Servant's Heart, and we should consider the service of others in our life's decision and actions."

Her hand now tightly gripped the cross. "I think that's why I loved Ron so much—he had the ultimate Servant's Heart—always putting others first. When he died—or how he died—

I always knew it could happen one day because he would never give up on saving someone else's life to protect his own." Her words dropped to a whisper, barely audible, as she stared straight ahead.

After several moments of silence, Matt suggested they take a minute to refill their coffees.

When they reconvened, Matt looked at Will. "What about you, Will?"

"I think that's what baseball did for me—gave me confidence. My buddies and I looked forward to the start of the season every year. It was a blast," Will shared.

"So it was fun, it helped with self-confidence, it was a place to fit in," Matt said. "As we're thinking about how to restart this season, I hope we can remember all those good things which came out of our own experiences. That's what we want to give our kids. And I think we can get there if we focus on each kid's needs and put some thought into how we build our program going forward. And I have a few ideas which should help us frame it all out."

B.J. smiled. "So where do we start? Should we look at the lineup? Map out practice?"

"Actually, I want to start with something else first," Matt said. "As coaches, we set the tone for the team. We're responsible for leadership and establishing the team culture. And it really helped me put this in perspective about a week ago when I figured out I had to understand my 'why'—why I am doing this."

He told them about why he started—because of friendship, because he wanted to get ready for the day when he could coach for his own kids—and how he ultimately came to understand the kids themselves are his 'why.'

"One night I realized my 'why' was those kids," he said. "I realized I needed to get my personal agenda out of the way and do this for the kids. I had to want to be a good influence on their lives. Help them see what the game has to teach them about life, maybe. And once I bought into the perspective we are here for all the kids, I became okay with the fact not all the parents are going to love what we are doing all the time, and probably half of them disagree with some aspect of the program or decisions we make."

The group chuckled collectively.

"But that's just part of coaching, we have a higher purpose here, and we have to be okay with it."

Will looked a little uneasy. "I'm really not that deep, if you want to know the truth. I just like the game, I like my kid and I like getting out of the house with Eli. And…yeah, okay…I have a hunch Eli might not get a minute in the game if I didn't show up to look out for him."

Matt nodded. "I suspect that's true for a lot of people who volunteer, Will."

Charlie and B.J. exchanged looks, their almost indiscernible nods acknowledging what Matt said.

"But that can't be all there is," Matt continued. "As much as I want all of you as part of the coaching team, I need you to know we don't need parents on the field—we need coaches."

Charlie nodded. "We'll be coaching all the kids. Not just our own."

"Exactly," Matt said. He watched as the four people around the table absorbed what had been said and began to nod. "There has to be something in this for each one of us besides how it benefits our own children. I don't expect you to know what your personal 'why' is tonight, but I do want you thinking about it. Is that fair?"

Everyone nodded.

"What about you, Matt? Is there something in it for you besides helping out a friend and making your wife happy?" B.J. asked.

Matt nodded. "I wasn't sure at first, but after letting this idea sink in for a while, I've realized this: If I'm a good coach, I'm going to learn as much as the kids I'm coaching. Heck, maybe more. A good coach has to be a leader, so in the process of becoming a better coach, I'm going to learn how to be a better husband, a better father and, in my case, a better business owner. I can see it already. I'm figuring out how to communicate better and get more out of the guys on my construction crews because of how I'm learning to communicate as a coach."

To give them all a chance to shift gears, Matt suggested they take a minute to refill their coffee. When everyone returned to the table, he said, "Okay. From what I heard, I think we all agree our "why" is focused on the kids, and making this a great experience for them. Now let's talk about everyone else, including me, you guys, all the parents, and everyone else who is exposed to the Bearcats for that matter."

They all started to nod. Although there were a couple puzzled glances exchanged.

"We need to agree upon our people strategy. It's our job, or let me rephrase that, it's MY job to establish the culture and set expectations for everybody. We are the leaders of this team, and as the leaders we need to describe what success means for the Bearcats."

"Here is something I have been thinking about and quite frankly, the more I think about it, the more I like it." Matt leaned forward and rested his elbows on the café table. "As individual players, and as a team, the Bearcats will be the very best we can be on the last day of the season, whenever that may be." Matt leaned back in his chair to give them a chance to think about what he'd said.

After a moment or two, Will frowned. "Shouldn't it say something about winning?"

"I think it does," Charlie said.

"What'd ya mean?" Will asked.

"Well, if all of the coaches, and each player focuses on continually improving every practice and every game, and the Bearcats truly are the best we can be on the last day of the season, for goodness sakes, we should have won a game or two along the way!"

The group shared a collective chuckle at that.

Charlie speculated. "Especially if we pay attention to what each kid really needs, work them hard but also make sure they are having fun doing it, we might be surprised where some of these kids can end up."

The smiling image of Luke's face flashed into Matt's head.

"But doesn't that just let them off the hook? Give them permission to lose?" Will asked.

"Not if we really stress we're expecting their best effort, execution, and some incremental improvement, win or lose," B.J. interjected. "And I also think we can connect it to playing together as a team, trusting each other, that kind of thing. Show them what it takes to be a leader on a team."

"A leader?" Will frowned. "Aren't they a little young to be talking leadership?"

Matt smiled. They definitely were tracking with the idea he'd brought to the table, and making it better through their input. Even Will, who was coming across as a Doubting Thomas, was making them all go deeper in their thinking because of his questions.

"I don't think so," Charlie said. "I think they'll get it if we can show them how it all works together to make a successful team. We have to believe in the program and trust it will work."

"Funny you should bring up trust, Charlie," Matt said. "I was just having a conversation about trust with someone, my mentor, this morning. Trust is the foundation for all of this, isn't it? We have to trust each other, and earn the trust of the kids."

"And their parents," said Sarah Kate. "If the parents don't trust us, we're never going to get anywhere with the kids."

B.J. nodded. "You realize the first place our coaching gets undermined is in the car on the way home, right?"

Matt shook his head. "Your exactly right, and I certainly understand it. This is a big time commitment for families, and everybody wants their kid to do well. If the parents don't understand what our program is trying to accomplish, there is no way we can expect their support. As coaches, we need to clearly communicate to all the parents and establish our culture, set the expectations, and get them on board with the success we want for their kids on multiple levels. We have to paint a picture of the benefits their kids might get from being part of the Bearcats, in addition to a trophy." Matt smiled and looked at his coaches. "'Cause that trophy's not looking too good at this point."

"Sure," Charlie said. "If the parents are feeding their kids messages that are different from the way we're coaching them, we're fighting an uphill battle. If you want to talk about establishing team culture, communication is critical."

Sarah Kate sat straight up in her chair as if a jolt of electricity had shot through her. "Matt, I was re-reading the email you sent to the parents last week, and how you made a short list of Parent expectations. They were clear, concise, easy to remember. I really don't see, as a parent myself, how anybody could argue with any of it."

"That's right Sarah Kate," Matt answered. And I have been told we need to make a similar list for the players which summarizes all of the things we are talking about. We will call it Player Rules."

"I can see that," Charlie said, thinking hard. "So we come up with a short list of phrases that could encompass all the things most important to the team? We could touch on values, outcomes, and how we interact with one another. We could define what success means for the Bearcats and work together to make progress against it. I like it!"

Sarah Kate beamed. "That really does say we are all about creating an experience for the kids. I like it, too. It's going to be a great experience for a kid like Luke, even if he never plays ball again."

"I'm in," B.J. said.

Will nodded. "Okay. I can buy into that too."

"Great. Let's keep moving forward," Matt said. "What does this say about the kind of team culture we want to create?"

"Each child is an important member of the team and can make a contribution," Sarah Kate said, smiling. "We just have to figure out what it is."

With a touch of skepticism, Will said, "Mason?"

"Hey, he did get on base the other night," B.J. said.

"That's right," Charlie said. "He launched the rally—and he just as easily could have been out."

"So part of what we have to figure out is how to develop them all—even a kid like Mason," Will echoed.

"And my Eli," B.J. added. "And kids like Gabe and Luke—they may be on the small side, but I personally believe we can find a way for them to be valuable to the team."

"Won't we be putting an awful lot of effort into kids who aren't going to win games for us?" Will asked. "Sounds like we could shortchange the kids who are good for the ones who...well, B.J. said it first...the kids who aren't really athletes."

"I heard a lot of discussion around that when I was playing college ball," Charlie said. "One of our coaches was a big believer in coaching up the bottom third of the team. You don't ignore the good players, obviously. But if you coach up the players who aren't strong early in the season, you're elevating the whole team for a big finish... hopefully."

Will shrugged. Matt could see he was struggling with some of these new ideas and hoped he would be able to get on board when all was said and done.

"So we're going to place as much value on the kids who aren't the stars as we do on the kids who look like our stars today," Matt said, noticing Sarah Kate was making notes on every key point. "That's part of our commitments as Bearcat coaches: coaching up the bottom third. What else?"

"It's 'our' team," B.J. said. *"Not my team. Our team."*

"Sold!" Matt said.

"But isn't it more than just saying it's our team?" Sarah Kate asked. "Shouldn't we do some other things which really make us unique? Things the kids will always remember when they think about being a Bearcat?"

"Like pizza night?" Charlie asked.

"Everybody does pizza night," Will said.

Matt sensed Sarah Kate had something more to say, but was hesitating. "Sarah Kate?"

"Well, I...this might seem silly..."

"Nothing's silly," B.J. said.

"Well, when I was a little girl, whenever one of us went the extra mile for something, my dad would say, 'Hey, Sarah Kate made an A on her test—sounds like we need a popsicle celebration.' Or, 'Hey, Bobby helped the neighbor next door bring her groceries in—doesn't that deserve a popsicle?' So it sort of made us feel like even small accomplishments were worth celebrating."

The way she smiled at the memory, everyone could tell it had made an impression she'd never forgotten.

"Popsicle night," Matt said. "I like it. Sarah Kate, how would you feel about making sure popsicle night happens once a week?"

She nodded, grinning. "I'd love to."

Now it was Will's turn to look a little uncomfortable. "I have another idea. Actually, you already did this before the last game, Matt. But I thought it was really smart."

"What's that?"

"When we huddled up before the game, the kids were kinda being their usual goof-off selves, not paying close attention and horsing around," Will said. "You could tell they weren't really listening to you. So instead of yelling at them to make sure they were listening—that's what I probably would've done—you started making them repeat what you were saying."

He went on to describe the way Matt had kept repeating the mantra about a fly ball translating into an out, drilling down on the phrase until the players were repeating it back to them.

"Lip loading," Charlie said.

"You mean that's a thing? It has a name?" Will said.

"Having some language that's unique to your team—what my old coach called 'lip loading.'" Charlie explained. "But with kids this age, I like what you did, Matt, getting them to repeat it until they owned the ideas, too."

"Great," Matt said. "Let's come up with a few key ideas we really want them to lock in on over the rest of the season. We'll do some lip loading with the kids, focusing on the things which will help them most."

They spent the next fifteen minutes coming up with mantras to incorporate into the unique language of the team.

"Okay, here's what we have," Sarah Kate said, glancing down at the notes she'd made. "In addition to 'Fly balls are outs,' we have: 'Put the ball in play and good things happen.' Also, 'Fast to first, smart to home.' 'Do the little things right.' 'Leaders bring energy.' 'Small ball wins big games.' 'Start with work, end with work.'"

The idea of repetition to drive home key points led naturally into a discussion about the importance of an efficient practice routine. Charlie, Will and B.J. agreed to spend some additional time mapping out a structure for practice. Charlie even offered to be available Saturday mornings for extra batting practice. Sarah Kate volunteered to work with Matt on communication to the parents. And Matt committed to working on his style of communication with the kids themselves, during huddles.

Matt was happy to see everybody was really stepping up.

"I have two more ideas for people strategy, before we move on to game strategy," Charlie said. "The coach is the coach."

B.J. said, "Meaning?"

"Meaning the coach—that's Matt—is the final word on the field, whenever we're out there where parents and kids are around," Charlie said. "The rest of us are a united front. What Matt says, goes. Especially when it comes to being the direct line of communication to parents. Parents don't get to make end runs around Matt by going through one of us. 'The coach is the coach.'"

"That'll take the heat off us," Will said. "How do you feel about that, Matt?"

"I think it makes sense. And you're right, it should take the heat off the rest of you so you can concentrate on the kids." Matt turned to Sarah Kate. "With the possible exception of you. As the team coordinator, you're naturally going to hear a lot from the parents."

"If I can go into those conversations remembering 'The coach is the coach,' I think it will help me," Sarah Kate said. "I can listen better, knowing it's not up to me to solve their problems. My job can be to remind them to talk to you when they have a real issue."

"Good." Matt smiled at everyone. "What's your second idea Charlie?"

"Well, since now we will have Player Rules and Parent expectations, why don't we make a third list for us, the coaches, and write down the stuff we're talking about right now, so we make sure the coaches stay on the same page? Then, in the heat of the battle, we'll have a standard we can hold each other accountable to." Charlie spoke as someone who had been there before.

"Perfect, let's do it." Will affirmed.

A big neon sign flashed in Matt head that read, "Coaching Commitments!" John had seemed pretty confident this meeting would go well, and he was right. That John is one smart old dude.

For the next hour, they hashed out the Player Rules and Coaching Commitments. Then they evaluated each player and how they could help each kid become their very best by the last day of the season. Charlie, Will and B.J. came up with a rough structure for the practice routine and decided how to split responsibilities. And they decided to focus on bunting as a high-priority skill for getting on base and on aggressive base running—including getting very good at stealing bases—as their game strategy for improving their win-loss record...their advantage...hopefully.

They wrapped up with a discussion about communication, including how Matt would communicate the restart to parents right away.

They left the coffee shop just as it was closing for the evening. Heading off in different directions to their cars, Charlie turned around and called out, "Hey, Coach! Good job!"

Matt realized it was the first time anyone had said that to him. But he was determined, for the sake of the kids, it wouldn't be the last.

### 

*Parents:*

*Thank you again for your support and patience with our rocky start to the season. I want to assure you positive changes are in the works!*

*First off, three parents have joined Will and me on the coaching staff.*

*Coaches B.J. and Charlie will be assisting us going forward; and Sarah Kate has volunteered to function as our Team Coordinator, handling logistics and team communications. Thanks for stepping up, everyone!*

*Second, what I want you to hear is the five of us spent this evening mapping out a plan to restart the season with the goal of finishing better than we started.*

*That's right: We're declaring a restart for the Bearcats!*

*We talked about why we are doing this. Unanimously, we agreed it is for the benefit of your kids, all of them. As coaches, we take this responsibility seriously and want them to have a great, positive experience, so that they absolutely want to come back and play again next year.*

*We decided our main outcomes for the season are summed up in the following statements:*

*You may remember from my last email a list parent expectations.*

- *We act with dignity.*
- *We maintain our perspective.*
- *We encourage all players on both teams.*
- *We use positive talk, cheer and encouragement only.*
- *Only the Head Coach addresses the officials or other teams' parents/coaches.*
- *Participate—get involved and be part of the solution, not part of the problem.*

*To round out the program for the Bearcats' success, we have added the following:*

## *Player Rules:*

- *We have fun.*
- *We do our best.*
- *We pay attention.*
- *We put teammates first.*
- *We show good sportsmanship.*
- *We are Servant Leaders.*
- *We will all be the best that we can be on the last day of the season.*

*And, so as not to feel left out, we created the following list for the Bearcat coaches and volunteers:*

## **Coaching Commitments:**

- *We are kind.*
- *We are present.*
- *We are positive.*
- *We are consistent.*
- *We trust and respect one another.*
- *We catch them doing something right.*
- *We coach them all.*

*Tomorrow night, we'll implement a new practice routine The focus will be on key fundamentals the kids need to learn that will help the Bearcats compete better.*

*You may receive emails directly from Sarah Kate, so be on the lookout for those; and you will want to tune in to our new Bearcats Facebook page for announcements and photos.*

*Of course, as the head coach, I'll continue to respond to any questions or concerns. Please bring them to me outside practice or game time, because we want to focus that time on your kids and the team.*

*Thank you for allowing us to work with your child. It is a privilege and an honor.*

*Coach Matt*

Matt wasn't nearly as nervous about this communication as he had been about the previous one. He felt confident he, Charlie, Sarah Kate, B.J. and Will were on the right track.

He just hoped this restart worked to turn things around for the Bearcats.

## Coach's Rule #6

*Set the tone and take the lead in establishing team culture for the players, coaches and parents. Know the coach is the coach.*

# CHAPTER 7:
# TEAM CULTURE

After Matt emailed the team parents about the restart, he didn't receive a single email from a parent. As he pulled into the gravel lot near the ball field for the next practice, Matt wondered what that meant. Had the parents given up? If so, how long would it be before the kids gave up, too? Then he remembered: I am there for the kids, and I have to be okay with whatever the parents think, both good and bad.

He received emails from all four of his assistant coaches, assuring him they were one hundred percent on board with the restart plan. Their words were enthusiastic and encouraging, and really boosted Matt's confidence they were doing the right thing.

Matt pulled gear out of his truck and headed for the dugout, feeling the way he sometimes felt when he started a new construction project that was completely different from anything he'd ever done before—excited by the possibilities but well aware failure was one possible outcome.

When the kids began to arrive and gather for the start of practice, they were as fidgety as ever, focused on everything but Matt—their shoes, their gloves, getting the bill of their ball caps folded just right. To capture their attention, Matt squatted so he was at eye level with them. Right away, the kids seemed to notice he was there, in front of them, in a way they hadn't when he was two feet above them.

"Listen up, Bearcats," he said, without even raising his voice the way he usually did to gain their attention. The players tilted their heads or leaned in a big closer to hear him. "We need to talk."

A couple of the kids who were usually inattentive cut their eyes in his direction, as if willing to give him a moment to fully capture their attention. Even Mason cocked his head in Matt's direction.

Matt spoke candidly. "We got off to a rough start this season. But we did win our last game, so the Bearcats have a 1-3 record. That's something to be proud of." He began to look each kid in the eyes. "But right now, as your coaches, we believe one of two things can happen."

Matt held up his index finger.

"One: We can continue practicing and playing the same way we've been and let the season keep playing out the way it is right now...and maybe, eventually, we'll start to win more. Or maybe we'll keep losing."

A few of the kids frowned.

Matt held up a second finger.

"Or, two: We can start over. And I mean completely over. The coaches and I think we have a plan which can make us a better team at the end of the season than we are right now." He paused, hoping that would sink in, not just for the kids but for any parents who were listening nearby, too. "But we will have to change the way we practice, so we're really working hard on the things which will make us better, and even introduce some new language to the team." Matt held up a piece of paper with the Player Rules in large print which all the players could easily read.

The kids looked at each other. A few looked over at their parents. Mason had stopped drawing circles in the dust.

"These are the Player Rules which we think can make a difference in the Bearcats. We will talk about them a little bit at each practice so we understand what they mean to us as teammates. The coaches will check in with the Player Rules to make sure that what we are doing is consistent with them. Paying attention, doing your best, having fun, are all things we can do, and are important to our team." Having the team's attention, Matt paused to let his words sink in.

Matt glanced at his coaching staff. Sarah Kate was smiling; Charlie nodded. "As your coaches, we want you to have a great experience. If we all work together, you will. Now the last rule is particularly important. Each of you take a minute and read it to yourself. Then you need to consider this question. Are you satisfied with how you're playing? Or, would you like to get a little better? If so, by working hard at every practice we can be the best team we can be at the end of the season.

"You mean it's up to us?" asked Zack.

"Well, we all need to agree—players and coaches," Matt said.

Brady kicked the dirt at his feet. "So we'll practice to win more?"

Matt looked Brady directly in the eyes. "We'll practice to get better, but we will also make sure we are treating each other well, working hard, and having some fun along the way. We will be building a team, in other words, and if we do that the right way, then yes, we should win more."

"We already practice a bunch," Hunter said.

"That's true," Matt said. "So the new coaching staff has spent some time looking at each one of you, figuring out what each one of you already does pretty well. From now on, we'll pay attention more closely to what each of you need, and drill you so you get better at those things."

The kids were now as engaged with him as he'd ever seen them. "Here's an example. We want to start coaching more of you on pitching, so we don't rely too much on one pitcher. Jermaine, Ethan and Jackson, we think you can pitch, but you need to learn the basic mechanics, so we're going to work with you on that. All of you are going to focus on bunting, because we think this is something which can give us an advantage in close games when we need to scratch out a run or two."

Jermaine grinned and swaggered around a bit, clearly already seeing himself as a star pitcher. A couple of the boys shrugged.

Hunter raised his hand. "So if we're starting over, does that mean our win last week doesn't count?"

"Great question, Hunter. The record stays the same. What's going to change is how we communicate and the way we practice, which hopefully will change the way we execute in the games. What do you all think?"

Zack glanced at his dad, then said, "Sure. Yeah. Let's do it. Definitely."

The only other response was the sound of Taylor thumping a ball into her glove with a wry smile on her face.

Finally Luke piped up and said, "Yeah! I do want to be better!"

Matt waited to see if there were any more responses. It didn't happen. "Okay, I want you to think about this during practice tonight."

Matt knew this was a lot to soak in for a bunch of ten year olds. And he hadn't earned the right to their enthusiasm, or their trust, just yet.

Matt stood to introduce B.J., Charlie and Sarah Kate and explain their new roles. Charlie had the kids count off by threes to break up into squads for stations and explained they would rotate every fifteen minutes. By the time Charlie had finished, Matt realized the kids' attention was starting to stray again. As the players shuffled off to practice, Matt checked his watch. They'd paid attention for about three minutes before their minds started to wander. Good to know.

It also dawned on him the kids really had started paying closer attention when he'd squatted to their level. Maybe he would try that again.

Relieved the first stage of restart was complete, Matt noticed Mason was lagging behind the others. When the other kids were out of earshot, Mason sidled up to Matt and said, so quietly Matt almost missed it, "Better. I vote for best we can be."

"That's great, Mason. I'm with you."

As Mason ambled in the direction of his practice squad, Matt sighed. Half-hearted agreement from Zack, enthusiasm from Luke and a vote of confidence from Mason. It was a start wasn't it?

### 

Practice looked better, thanks to the coaches and almost in spite of the kids. They stuck with the routine they'd planned and kept it moving. B.J. focused on pitching and catching. Charlie gave them batting practice, including introducing the bunt, while Will worked on base running. If Matt didn't have what it took to inspire the kids, maybe these coaches had what it would take to teach them. It looked organized, it looked like the coaches had a plan, and it looked like the kids were paying more attention than usual. Maybe it was just the novelty of doing something different. Maybe it would be hard to maintain focus beyond this one practice. He didn't know. But for the moment, he felt a small measure of hope.

He decided to hang onto that attitude as long as he could.

Matt moved from station to station, learning the coaching techniques each coach was using and paying attention to how the players were responding. About halfway through the practice, Charlie came over to Matt and said, "I have an idea. Might seem a little far-fetched, but what do you think about trying Mason behind the plate?"

"Catcher? He won't even hit. What makes you think he'll catch?"

"I was watching him during practice. He gets really dialed in when the ball is coming at him. A lot of Aspy kids are like that—something specific seems to rivet their attention. Sometimes it's music or math or video games. For Mason, I think it's the ball. I'm wondering if the bat gets in the way, confuses him. But he seems really comfortable with the glove." Charlie shrugged. "My gut just tells me this is something we should try."

"Great. Give it a shot." Matt gestured toward the current catcher. "What about Jermaine? I know we're going to try him as pitcher. But when he isn't pitching?"

"I'll plug him in at short stop and maybe center field. He's athletic and has a strong arm."

"Okay. Let's do it."

At the end of practice, the team huddled again and Matt introduced one more new element of the practice routine for their season restart: conditioning. From now on, he said, they could play and horse around until five minutes before practice, then they would do a quick warm up, jog a lap, and do a base-running routine. After this, while the kids were huffing and puffing, the coaches would huddle up to check in and go over the practice plan for the day. Then they would start practice. At the end of practice, there would be five more minutes of conditioning. Start with work, end with work.

"Starting next week, you'll know the routine and you'll jump right in. Even if none of us coaches are here, you'll know what to do. Got it?" Everyone nodded. "So every practice starts with work, and ends with work."

Matt saw a few wandering eyes and said, "Start with work, end with work. Let me hear you. Start with work…"

"End with work," came the listless response from a few members of the team.

"Once more. Start with work…"

"End with work." Louder if not necessarily more enthusiastically. Matt decided not to push it.

"Now there's one more thing," he said, gesturing to Sarah Kate, who began to roll a cooler into position behind the dugout. "Every Thursday, if we have a good practice, it's going to be Popsicle Thursday. And since we're doing a lot of things different starting tonight and all of you have put in a lot of effort, why don't you get over there and grab a popsicle."

That, at least, generated some enthusiasm. The kids ran for Sarah Kate, who grinned as she handed out the popsicles. She even brought enough for siblings, parents and coaches to have a popsicle. For about ten minutes, everybody stood around eating popsicles. People began to loosen up and chat. The mood around the Bearcats' dugout felt almost like they were a team.

Matt gave Sarah Kate a thumbs-up, and while he was doing so noticed she was handing out a small laminated card to each player. The kids shoved the cards in their back pockets as they continued to laugh and chomp on their popsicles.

After everyone else had cleared out, Matt called the coaches over. "What did you think? How'd it go? On a scale of one to ten, how was practice?"

"About a seven tonight," Charlie said. "Which is way better than it's been."

"We've been about a two," B.J. said. "I agree with Charlie."

"I liked the progress we made," Charlie said. "I think we have some kids who can bunt for a hit, like the younger guys, plus Luke, Taylor, Hunter, and even Ethan, if he can stop being a showboat. This may turn out to be our brilliant big idea for the season. Bunt defense is pretty complicated, and it isn't something most teams spend a lot of time practicing. So it could really disrupt the other team's game."

"Good. Let's try to make that a solid advantage for us," Matt said.

Charlie nodded. "Sure thing, Coach."

"I was thinking," Will added, "maybe I could be here an hour early Saturday morning, in case any of the kids want to practice base running before the game."

Matt encouraged him to give it a try and promised to send out an email to the parents letting them know.

"I can post an announcement on the Facebook page, too, if that's okay," Sarah Kate said.

"Perfect."

"And I got a couple of really fun shots after we handed out the popsicles. I could post them, too."

Matt nodded. "Have we had many families sign up for the page?"

"All but one, I think—I haven't seen Hunter's parents. And we've had a few grandparents, too. And I took it upon myself to create some cards with our new Player Rules on them, and handed them out tonight."

"Excellent! Sarah Kate, you're on a winning streak even if the team isn't. Popsicle Night was a hit, too." Matt made a mental note to go over the Player Rules with the kids again at the next practice.

"Thanks, Matt."

"So what are our do-betters?" Matt asked. "What do we need to adjust next time?"

They spent a few more minutes talking about ways to engage the kids who already played fairly well without losing focus on the kids who still needed help to really contribute to the team.

As they wrapped up, Matt said, "Thank you. All of you. Thanks for thinking we can do this. I think we've started to set a solid foundation for the team. Now let's see how we look in the next game."

### 

As the game began two nights later, Matt was feeling, if not confident, at least hopeful.

The huddle up before the game felt better. Some of the kids were paying more attention. They had adopted the new mantras he'd introduced—especially "Small ball wins big games"—in addition to the one he'd used before the previous game, "Fly balls are outs."

The kids were enthusiastic and loud in their responses by the time he said, "Okay, one more thing tonight. We're not going to straggle out onto the field any more. We're going to go out together, as a team."

Hunter and Jermaine tapped knuckles.

"Here's how we're going to do that," Matt said. "When it's time to take the field, at the beginning of the game and during each inning, I want you to huddle up in front of the dugout. We'll take about thirty seconds to get focused, then everybody will run—not walk—to their position."

That's what they did, ending by calling out in unison, "Bearcats!" before they sprinted onto the field. Matt thought they looked pretty sharp in their blue uniforms with the red trim and the purposeful way they moved. A few parents noticed the difference in the beginning and there was scattered applause.

As Matt left the dugout, he noticed Taylor had taken one of the laminated cards Sarah Kate had passed out and clipped it to the chain link fence. It was one of the Player Rules cards Sarah Kate had made for each player.

*Awesome*, thought Matt, pleased with this added sign of Taylor's leadership. He made a note to praise her in front of the team in a future huddle.

They lost a bit of their concentration as the game wore on, and things inevitably went wrong. Jermaine made several wild throws from short stop which could have been outs. Gabe missed a fly ball but then caught it quickly on the first hop and threw it to Jermaine in time to keep a runner from advancing. Jackson was wild when they gave him a turn as the pitcher late in the game. If he could learn Taylor's control, he would be a real plus in the rotation.

The surprise of the game proved to be Mason.

Just as he had perfected the batting stance, he also looked solid when he settled in behind the home plate as catcher. Matt was sweating bullets the entire first inning, but Mason caught the pitches with ease and threw them back to Taylor with precision. He fumbled around the first time a runner came sliding into home plate, the unexpected play causing him some confusion about what he was supposed to do next. By the time he refocused, the runner was safe.

Mason redeemed himself in the final inning of the game, however.

In the top of the inning, the other team had runners on second and third with only one out. Matt was beginning to fear this could end up as another rout. The score was 8-2 and, if both players in scoring position made it home, the Bearcats would once again end the game with an opponent scoring in double digits. He could tell the Bearcats were dejected but still paying attention and engaged.

Mason continued to be riveted on the game.

The batter bunted. The player at third was heading home. Given the Bearcats' reputation for a slack defense, it should have been an easy run, with another player advancing into scoring position.

Mason pounced and barehanded the baseball and tagged the runner coming home.

Then, with quick thinking which stunned everyone, Mason wheeled and threw the ball to Zack at first base. A double play to end the inning!

The Bearcats' side of the field went wild. And when the players started the second half of the final inning, they were so jazzed Brady and Ethan scored two more runs, for a final score of 8-4, a big improvement over 10-2. This game went into the loss column, but to Matt it felt like a victory.

And when the team huddled after the game, they were almost as excited as if they had won the game.

Matt knelt on one knee and the kids immediately settled down to see what he had to say—another small win as far as Matt was concerned.

"So what do you think, Bearcats? Did we play better today?"

The kids on the team who were beginning to step up as enthusiastic leaders—Taylor, Zack, Luke and Eli—were joined by Jackson and Jermaine in a resounding, "Yes!"

"We put the ball in play and good things happened! Let's remember that. Put the ball in play and..."

"Good things happen!"

"Exactly. Remember, this is a personal win for us even if the game doesn't go in the win column." Ethan and Hunter responded with knuckle raps. "I want to give kudos to Mason for the quick thinking on the double play. That was really an awesome MVP move if I ever saw one. And in the last inning, Hunter's RBI line drive scored Brady and Ethan. In fact, every single one of you made a contribution today and we kept the energy up all the way to the end. Great job, everybody!"

Matt looked around at the players. "We're going to hear from the other coaches in a minute, but I'm wondering what you have to say about today's game. Anything you see we can improve or anybody you want to tip your cap to?"

They were silent for a moment, then Taylor said, "I thought Mason did a great job catching today."

"Absolutely," Matt said. "Way to be a great teammate, Taylor."

Jermaine said, "I liked being in the outfield."

"I only dropped the ball once," Eli chimed in. "'Cause we're catchers, not droppers."

Matt smiled as the grinning boy repeated one of the things he'd learned during practice. "Good job, Eli! Anything else?"

Gabe, another one of the smallest kids on the team, said, "Nobody messed up real bad today."

Everybody laughed.

"Good point, Gabe," Matt said. "And we did the little things right. How about you, coaches? What stood out for you today?"

"It looked like you had a lot of fun today, and really paid attention the whole game. And as Eli said, you were catchers, not droppers today," B.J. said. "All together, you caught three fly balls!"

Matt led in a round of applause.

"I want to say everybody kept their cool when we were down, and that was really good," Charlie said. "We let our energy drop in the middle innings, but we rallied. We need to work on keeping our energy high the entire game even if we're down by a few runs. Remember, leaders bring energy!"

"Good point, Coach Charlie," said Matt. "Let's keep that in mind: Leaders bring energy!"

Matt touched on the idea of each player, and the entire team, being the very best they could be on the last day of the season. He led them in a final team cheer, and everyone began to disperse. As they walked away, Matt could tell it really had been a victory today, no matter what the scoreboard said. For the first time, he felt like he might make a go of this coaching thing after all.

## Coach's Rule #7

*Establish language that reinforces the program, and speak it often.*

# CHAPTER 8:
# WINNING

The euphoria of seeing so much progress barely lasted long enough for Matt to get home. As he pulled his pickup into the driveway, his phone beeped with a text from Sarah Kate.

*Not all parents happy w/game. Don't like changes in player positions, feel ur not hitting hard on winning.*

Under his breath, Matt muttered his own little expression of unhappiness. Then, as he entered the kitchen, he told himself not to let the few who might complain disturb his peace of mind.

"You're just in time to read a bedtime story, if you're up for it," Traci said with her usual bright smile as she leaned in to give him a welcome home kiss. "How'd it go?"

"Depends on who you talk to, apparently," he said, hugging her. "And I'd love to read a story."

Maelee was eating her banana and in an excited, chatty mood so reading her bedtime story took almost forty-five minutes before her eyes began to drift shut. Matt loved being part of this ritual of putting their two-year-old daughter to bed. He loved the cherry vanilla bubble-bath scent of her. He loved her plump pink cheeks and her deep blue eyes and the soft red curls were going to be just like her mother's one day. He loved answering her questions about the puppy dog and the way she giggled over certain strings of words in the story.

So by the time Maelee was asleep, Matt was back in a mellow mood and ready to relax on the sofa with Traci. He kissed the top of her head and said, "Let me check email and make sure everything is lined up for work tomorrow. I'll be right back."

"Are you going to tell me a bedtime story?" Traci asked playfully.

"You bet I will," he said.

Matt turned on the small desk lamp and fired up his laptop. As soon as he opened the email, he knew he should just shut it down and walk away. There were four emails from parents, three with the subject line: WINNING!

Obviously they had been talking to each other and intended to send him a clear message.

*Coach (and I use the term loosely) I understand from my son Brady you are encouraging him to BUNT instead of swinging away. Brady has it in him to be a champion. He can do so much better than BUNT! If you can't give my son the coaching he needs to unleash his batting capabilities, I may be forced to look for a better team for him.*

*Like losing Brady would make or break the team,* Matt thought. The freckle-faced boy had some skills worth developing, but first he needed to start taking the practices and games seriously, as well as lose a little bit of his conviction that he deserved to be the star of the team. It was clear from the email where the boy got his attitude.

The next email was from Jermaine's father.

*I understand you have demoted my son from catcher to the outfield. No wonder you are still losing.*

Matt sighed heavily. He hoped Jermaine's dad would come to understand Jermaine had real potential to shine if he became the answer to catching the fly balls which were killing them, as well as getting him into the rotation as a pitcher. And Jermaine himself had said he liked playing outfield.

Next up, an email from Gabe's father. Gabe was one of the two smallest kids on the team.

*I thought you should know (which you would, if you were paying attention) some of the bigger boys make fun of Gabe, who is well within the normal range for his age. Baseball players do not have to be massive, you know! My wife and I feel it is a big part of your responsibility to teach good sportsmanship.*

*Ouch!* Matt thought. If teasing or bullying were going on, Gabe's father was dead on. It was Matt's responsibility to put an end to it. He kept reading.

*Also, after practice last week, Gabe said you told them the Bearcats were not going to lose anymore. Well, you certainly lost tonight. Gabe did not seem upset, but I think it is wrong of you to mislead these kids. Where did you get your training as a coach? If these were your kids, you would surely be trying a little harder to make them look good out there.*

Matt rubbed his forehead. He had tried hard to express the coaching staff's position about making improvements as the pathway to winning in the email he'd sent to parents. He wondered if Gabe's dad had even read it. Matt believed the kids understood what he and the other coaches were saying about becoming better as part of their game plan to win some games. Matt could understand confusion on the part of the kids; but based on these emails, he had not done a very good job of communicating to the parents.

*The coach is the coach,* he reminded himself. Clearly, he needed to do some follow-up communication and manage their expectations a little better.

The final email was from Taylor's dad. The pitcher was one of his better players; he dreaded whatever lambasting he might be about to receive from her father.

> *Hey, Coach, just wanted to say thanks for all you're doing for our kids. Taylor always has an upbeat attitude, but all the losing was starting to get to her. After practice this week and tonight's game, she was not down at all. I think she was even a little excited. Somehow, you've helped her see all losses are not created equal— and progress is a victory. Anyway, just wanted to let you know her mom and I appreciate what you're doing for the kids in trying to turn this season around.*

Matt closed his eyes, grateful for that little ray of sunshine. He tried to convince himself that most of the parents he hadn't heard from were happy with the changes and understood what he and the other coaches were trying to achieve. Or maybe they were just fuming quietly or complaining behind the scenes.

Answering those emails had to be his top priority, and he was immediately grateful for the standard emails Sarah Kate had helped him draft. He sent a quick thank you to Taylor's parents, then pulled up the "complaint" email response:

> *Thank you so much for caring enough about your child's experience with the Bearcats to write with your questions and feedback.*

He hesitated over the next sentence, but knew it was part of his commitment as coach.

*I want to invite you to meet with me at Full o' Beans coffee shop at 7 p.m. Wednesday night so I can hear you out. Your child is important to me. I look forward to seeing you there.*

*Not.* But at least, thanks to the communication Sarah Kate had crafted, his irritation didn't show.

*You're doing this for the kids,* he reminded himself. *Get your ego out of the way and do what's best for the kids.*

He couldn't wait for morning. He needed to talk to *his* coach, John.

### 

John's renovations were almost completed. The kitchen had been finished. Today, the ramp to the deck was coming off. By end of day, the project would be done.

"I think we need to add a third story," Matt quipped as he and John sat at the kitchen table sipping their coffee. "Otherwise, I'm going to miss out on all this coaching and run the Bearcats into the ground."

John laughed heartily. "As happy as I am with the work your crew has done, I think I'm going to pass on the addition."

"I figured you'd say that."

"But I thought things were starting to look up after the restart," John said. "The kids made some good plays last night. At least, that's how it looked from where Buster and I were sitting."

"I guess it looks a little different from the viewpoint of parents who think their kids are the center of the universe and don't like change if they think it isn't in their own child's best interests."

"Still getting some negative pushback?"

"Four emails waiting for me when I got home last night."

"Any of them positive?"

"One."

John shook his head. "Well, at least there's one."

"The three negative parents all had an ax to grind. They all started with subject line 'WINNING'—I guess they got together on that—but basically telling me how their kids weren't getting a fair shake." Matt absent-mindedly picked up his coffee cup, then set it back on the table. "Bottom line, I guess I still need to do a better job of communication."

"When you communicated the restart, what did you say about winning?"

"Yeah, that's the problem. I didn't say much about winning."

"Ah."

"So what did you do last night?"

"Used one of the standard emails Sarah Kate helped me write to invite them to meet me Wednesday night so I can hear them out."

"Looking forward to that, I'm sure," John said with his usual wry tone.

"Oh, yeah."

"And what are you going to say? You going to tell them they're all wrong?"

"Not a good idea, I suppose."

"Maybe not. Especially for the ones who aren't your biggest fans."

"I could tell them if they aren't happy with the way things are going they might want to go ahead and take their kids out." Matt spotted the slight change in John's expression, a deepening of the crease in his forehead that usually meant he didn't like something he was hearing. "Okay. Also not the best approach. But I can't just give them a bunch of rah-rah, tell them to hang in there, that we're going to get better. I mean, we *are* going to get better. But that doesn't mean we're going to finish the season with a winning record. So what do I tell them that's not misleading? Should I be rethinking this restart?"

There was a long silence. John finally stood, went to the counter to refill their coffee mugs, scratched Buster behind his ears, then sat down. "A good coach can't flap in the wind."

"What do you mean?"

"I mean, you and your team of coaches worked out a plan. Now work that plan. You have to stay the course, give it a chance to make a difference." John gave him a long, steady look. "I can guarantee one thing."

"What's that?"

"If you start tinkering with the plan after every game—or worse, after every complaint—you won't be any better off at the end of the season. You'll probably be worse."

Matt found it hard to imagine being any worse.

"Matt, you can't fool yourself into thinking you're going to start winning right away. Or even you'll be one of the top teams by the end of the season."

"I know, but—"

"You're not going to be a Tony LaRussa, you know, or a Joe Torre."

"Yeah, I know."

They sat in silence for a few minutes.

"What do you believe about winning, Matt?"

"You mean for these kids?"

"I mean in your core. What is winning all about to you? Is winning just what shows up on the scoreboard?"

What *does* winning mean for me? "That's kind of a big question," Matt responded.

"Yes. Yes, it is." John looked him squarely in the eye. "What you believe about winning becomes what you teach your players. And that stands a good chance of becoming a core belief those kids will carry with them through life. Yep, that's kind of a big question. Deserves some serious thought, don't you think?"

### 

Matt sat at a front table in Full o' Beans, his eyes on the front door, wondering who might show up. He almost hoped nobody would. He wasn't looking forward to this. But he knew trying to build bridges with these disgruntled parents was going to be critical to his ability to turn around the Bearcats. He was really mindful of what Charlie had said about parents being able to dismantle all their coaching efforts with the kids on the drive home after a game. He needed to do his best to get these parents on board with the program.

The first parent through the door was Gabe's dad, a feisty looking man still wearing his button-down blue shirt from the office. Matt greeted him and tried to make small talk while they waited for the other parents. Soon, the fathers of Brady and Jermaine came through the door, spotted them and headed for the counter. They ordered coffee and joined Matt.

"Thanks for taking me up on my offer and coming out to talk tonight," Matt said.

"Ethan's dad is coming, too," said Brady's father.

"Good," Matt said, telling himself there was no reason to feel angry or threatened. Sure, he supposed they could fire him if they wanted to, but so what?

So what? So Matt cared about their kids and the plans the coaches had worked up.

More small talk. A few more minutes of waiting. Ethan's dad came.

*Four against one,* Matt thought, then reminded himself this wasn't a contest. Or was it?

"Let's cut to the chase," as Ethan's dad, who introduced himself as Frank said, immediately making his play to run the meeting. "We know you took this on after your buddy bailed and we're just not sure..." He looked around at the other fathers. "We're just wondering. That's all."

Matt decided to see what the other dads had to say before he decided how to make his case.

"Thank you for being frank with me." No response. Tough crowd. "Ok then, what would the rest of you like to add?" He looked at them one by one. Only Gabe's father looked him in the eye.

"It just seems to us you don't have a good handle on what to do with this bunch of kids," Gabe's father said, using a corporate-speak tone of voice that felt condescending to Matt, who was also still dressed from work—but not in a button-down shirt and necktie. "And you aren't a father yourself. Maybe this is a job better suited to a parent."

Matt bit his tongue.

"I didn't know that," Frank, Ethan's father, said. "So you're not a coach **or** a parent? How did this happen?"

Jermaine and Brady's fathers just sat and looked at Matt, obviously waiting for an answer.

"I'm glad you're raising these issues," Matt said, keeping his tone as even and friendly as possible. "I can see I haven't done a very good job of communicating. I really appreciate the chance to hear your expectations because ten parents may have ten different sets of expectations. One of the toughest things about coaching this team—any team, really—is figuring out how to reconcile all the different expectations and get to a place which works for everybody."

Frank and the other fathers exchanged skeptical glances.

"So I'd like to start by asking each of you, what is most important to you as a parent of one of our players?"

The other three looked to Frank first. He said, "I want what's best for my kid. Ethan's got a lot of potential and I want him to have good coaching."

Matt nodded, then looked at the other three fathers. They were nodding.

"I want Jermaine to get more playing time in the infield and at catcher. And I want him to feel what it's like to win some games."

Brady's father said, "I just want him to have some fun. The way I had fun when I was a kid." He glanced at Frank and shrugged.

Gabe's dad looked Matt squarely in the eye and said, "I want my boy to learn being little isn't the end of the world. I want him to figure out he has a shot in sports, if he applies himself."

Matt let those different viewpoints sink in. "Those are great things to know. Thanks. I know the other coaches will really benefit from hearing what's important to you."

The four fathers still looked less than sold on Matt's response.

"Now let me answer some of your earlier questions," Matt said. "First, I want to assure you I *am* a father, although my daughter isn't yet old enough to play. And I do have some coaching experience from my college days. I helped out with the local high school. But more importantly, two of the coaches in charge of instruction for your sons have significant playing and coaching experience. I sent their introductions out with the email about restarting the season. I can re-send it if you missed it. And they have kids on the team."

All the dads, except Frank, sank back in their chairs, almost like balloons that were slowly losing air. The only one who remained tense and ready to speak up was Frank.

"One good thing about that, of course, is I bring balance because I'm not committed to any *one* of your kids." Matt continued before Frank could speak up, "I'm committed to *all* of them. And the coaches have all committed to instructing your kids as diligently as if they're coaching their own. That's one of the values we've committed to as a coaching staff, which is good for your kids."

"Well, that's all well and good," Frank started, "but that doesn't seem to be resulting in a better team. You're just moving our kids around willy-nilly and not really thinking through what is best for them."

"We've actually been very intentional about evaluating the players to see where they might bring the most value to the team," Matt said firmly, realizing Frank was giving it his best effort to intimidate and sway the thinking of the other fathers. "And we're highly focused on coaching the bottom third of the team as well as the top third of the team. That's going to elevate the entire team."

"But my boy is a good catcher," Jermaine's father protested.

That wasn't actually true, but Matt knew better than to say so. "Jermaine really likes outfield—he is athletic and covering ground seems to suit him. And the Bearcats need an agile player who can make those plays in center field for us. Plus, we think he has the potential to be one of our pitchers."

"Pitcher?" Jermaine's father looked surprised. "He didn't tell me that. I just thought you were shuffling him off to the outfield."

"Not at all," Matt said. "He's a very valuable player. And he seems to be enjoying himself a lot more now he's not locked into one spot behind the plate."

Jermaine's father nodded and looked at Ethan's father; they were obviously buddies.

Frank cleared his throat. "Well, okay, but what's this business about getting Ethan to bunt instead of hit. He's a good hitter! Why would you have him doing a sacrifice bunt?"

"That's a great question. Bunting is going to be a big part of our game strategy," Matt said, leaning into the table. "None of the teams in the league spend a lot of time coaching defense against bunting. So bunting is a great way for us to disrupt the other teams and get on base. As for Ethan, he has shown enough control and judgment as a hitter that we think he'll be a good leader and set an example for the other kids. He'll be hitting, too, of course, as well as learning to bunt and growing as a team leader."

That's how B.J. explained the decision to Matt and he was glad to see it seemed to make sense to Frank, too.

"You see, all these are strategies for developing the whole team. We think that's how everybody gets better—and how we get to a better record before the season is over. We believe that establishing a culture where every kid is being coached to improve and the kids enjoy being there—will lead to wins. We're not doing these things in lieu of winning. This is *how* we're going to win."

They talked for another half hour and, by the time they were ready to wrap up the discussion, most of the fathers were in a better frame of mind.

"Listen," Matt said. "I really do appreciate your concerns and I want you to know I want to hear from you any time. And thanks to your feedback, I'm going to do a better job communicating with the parents."

When they stood up to leave, only Gabe's father hung back, loosening his necktie. When they were alone, Gabe's dad said, "Thanks for your time, Matt. But I still wanted to mention the whole bullying thing. Gabe's not a big kid, and I worry some of the bigger kids are making it harder on him."

"The other coaches and I take that very seriously," Matt said. "I promise you, we're going to deal with it. And I want you know, I want to hear about anything at all you hear from Gabe. He's a good kid and I want this to be a great experience for him."

They shook hands and headed out to their cars.

As he drove home, Matt felt far better than he had when the evening began. He really felt he'd changed a few minds. He hoped he wasn't just kidding himself.

### 

With practice coming up the next evening, Matt knew he had to communicate to the parents before he had another talk with the team.

All day, as he traveled from work site to work site, Matt replayed the meeting with those four fathers the night before and thought long and hard about John's questions. *What do you believe about winning? What is winning all about?*

He knew, as he was sure John had intended, these were big questions which deserved more than a simple, carelessly-delivered message.

Deciding what he believed about winning was central to his success as a coach. It would become, as John had boldly declared, one of the main things he would teach the kids on the team. A thing that went way beyond batting and running and catching. Way beyond working together as a team, even.

What they learn about winning can shape the way they see the world and their place in it.

Winning touched every area of life. How they viewed winning could impact the way they conducted themselves in high school—which would arrive for these ten-year-olds in a few short years—in college, in their careers, even when they started their own families years down the road.

*Yep. You're in over your head.* He could only hope he did the right thing for the kids.

That afternoon between jobs, he stopped at the Full o' Beans and used his laptop to write about winning until he felt he was clear. When he finished, he sent his draft to the coaches.

He needed to be sure they were onboard before he communicated to the parents that night.

### ###

*Parents:*

*I've heard from some of you about the changes we've made to restart the Bearcats' season. I want to thank everyone who gave me their thoughts.*

*Some of you specifically asked about winning.*

*Right now, we are 1-4 for the season, which does not look much like a winning season. So I wanted to make sure you all understand something:*

*We have not given up on these kids, or on this season.*

*These changes we're making aren't in lieu of winning.*

*These changes are how we intend to win.*

*And in addition to winning on the scoreboard, we aspire for your children to have success at multiple levels.*

*We have an opportunity with these kids to teach them many important lessons. The steps we take to respond as a team to our current situation may be something they can use in the future, in all areas of their lives. We have to take what this season has given us, and make it work. Hopefully, these things will lead us to winning…at least more than we have so far.*

*So let's be clear, we are not giving up on the idea of winning some games with this team.*

*Here's how we see winning:*

*Winning is a worthy ideal. It is the reason we keep score. There is nothing wrong with winning every game, for those who can, but there are other important ways besides the final score for children to measure success. We have to find those ways for this group, during this season. We have to define some wins in terms we, and we alone control, so regardless of what our final record is, these kids can feel good about this team, this season and the progress made.*

*In addition to the scoreboard, here are some other wins we are going for:*

*Continuous improvement – The players, coaches and team will be the very best we can be on the last day of the season, whenever that is for us.*

*Culture – We want to have fun, be good sports and great teammates.*

*Come back – We want all the kids to have positive experiences so they desire to return to play baseball again next year, on this team, or any other.*

*We can't always control all the factors that result in the final score of the game. But these are success markers we can control.*

*Charlie, Will, B.J., Sarah Kate and I understand it's our job to put your children in the best possible position to win. We commit to doing that. And again, we want your kids to win on many levels.*

*We hope you'll be onboard with letting us coach your children to be winners, no matter what the final score says. Because we believe if we do that, the scores will inevitably get better.*

*Coach Matt*

## Coach's Rule #8

*Define multiple measures of success around outcomes you control.*

# CHAPTER 9:
# GAINING AN EDGE

Go figure. The kids on the team loved the idea of learning to be a team of successful bunters. So Matt and the other coaches decided to get equally focused on giving them another advantage —aggressive base running. Specifically, stealing bases. Kids this age can steal bases, but they needed to learn how to read a pitcher's moves to know when to steal. Charlie was going to teach them that.

"Okay, Bearcats! We're going to do something fun tonight," Matt said after the kids had let off some steam and taken charge of their own drills at the beginning of practice. He squatted to their level. "We're going to learn to get really good at stealing bases. And that's going to help us score more runs."

A few of the kids laughed, and those who liked the idea of being a hero by stealing bases cheered.

By combining bunting with base stealing and other aggressive base-running moves, the coaches felt the Bearcats could gain just enough edge to score a few extra runs—which coupled with a much improved effort, attitude, and other rapidly developing skills, might be all they needed to break into the win column a little more often.

In the interest of gamification—turning practice drills into games—Charlie and B.J. were going to implement a bunting competition during practice. They also were going to lead some extra practices related to the nuances of bunting and stealing: focusing on bunting by a couple of left-handed hitters—Brady and Gabe—who would already be two steps closer to first base; teaching the art of the secondary lead for base running; and recognizing when the pitcher was committed to a going home with the pitch.

By the end of the practice, the coaches felt very clear bunting and improved base running could be a real advantage.

The main thing was the kids began to understand the need to run the bases aggressively. They were grasping the idea they all needed to run hard and run smart —a notion that was new for some of the kids who didn't have much experience.

"I think we'll see a difference at our next game," Charlie told Matt when practice was over.

"Yeah? You think it's going to work?"

Charlie grinned. "It can't hurt. Who are we playing next?"

"The Screaming Eagles."

Charlie groaned. The Screaming Eagles were mostly a second-year team with a lot of talent and a reputation for being bullies. They weren't the best team in the league, but they were close.

"Actually, that may be perfect," Matt said. "We can't expect to beat them, so if we get in practice against them, maybe we'll be more prepared for the next game."

"Who's that?" B.J. asked.

"The Crushers."

"Oh, boy," Will said.

"I know," Matt agreed. "They're big and they're tough."

The Crushers also had one of the most respected coaches in the league. The best Matt felt he could hope for was that the team wouldn't be humiliated against either the Screaming Eagles or the Crushers.

After everyone else had drifted off to their cars, the last person in the ball park besides Matt was John, with his ever-present sidekick, Buster.

"How's the remodeled house?" Matt asked as he gathered up equipment to haul back to his truck.

"Like it," John responded, rousing Buster from his nap. "Your boys did a good job. I'm missing the morning coffee, though. Might have to install some stairs up to the attic or something."

Matt laughed. "I miss it, too. Maybe we need to keep the coffee time, minus the stairs you don't need."

"Sounds good."

John and Buster walked with Matt to his truck.

"You run a good practice these days," John said as Matt shoved the equipment into the truck bed.

"Thanks. I appreciate that. It's mostly Charlie and B.J. They really know what they're doing." He faced the old guy whose face had become as familiar as any family member over the last month. "I owe that to you, Coach."

John waved his hand dismissively. "Before a coach can do you one bit of good, you have to be coachable."

"Losing makes you coachable in a hurry."

John chuckled. "Maybe so. But you're learning. And the kids are starting to look good out there."

"Yeah. We've got two tough teams coming up, though. I hope it's going to be enough."

"Enough for what?"

Matt realized exactly what John was getting at: He still had to resist the urge to think it was all about the score. He nodded and smiled at the old man who had taught him so much, who still had so much to teach him.

"I hear ya," he said, even though John hadn't really said a thing. "Enough for these kids to gain a little more confidence in themselves, maybe."

"You might get surprised Matt. Funny things tend to happen when a baseball team finds some confidence and plays fast, loose, and happy."

Matt shook his head. "Need a lift?"

John looked down at Buster, who had already settled down for a nap in the few minutes they'd been standing by the truck. "Why not? Buster looks like he's all done with walking today."

Driving down Main Street, Buster curled up on the seat between them, Matt noticed one of his players, Hunter, trailing down the sidewalk after a group of older boys who kept turning on him. They didn't look threatening, exactly, but Matt could tell by the expression on their faces that they were teasing him.

Seeing Hunter struggling to fit in, he made up his mind to talk to the boy.

As if reading his mind—or perhaps just following his gaze—John asked, "How are the kids doing with all the changes?"

"For the most part, they're rolling with it fine. It feels like the kids are happy as long as they're having fun."

"You know, people need a lot less than they think to be happy, and to feel good about themselves," John said. "One of the things we all need is the belief we are making progress toward something that matters." And after a few seconds John added, "Sometimes a coach's toughest challenge is overcoming messages kids are getting in other parts of their lives."

### 

During movie night at home with Traci and Maelee that evening, Matt couldn't shake John's words. Once again, John seemed to have zeroed in on a lesson about something that had never occurred to Matt.

He thought about the boys who were the biggest challenges for the team—not kids like Luke or Eli or Gabe or Mason, but kids like Hunter and Ethan and Jermaine. All three boys showed signs they weren't receiving the attention they needed elsewhere in their lives. They clowned around to get attention. They picked on others to make themselves feel better. They didn't give the game their full attention or effort, but they wanted to be the MVP.

Who knew what kinds of problems they faced away from the game?

Matt looked at Maelee, giggling over the animated Disney flick. She was getting the very best he and Traci could give her. And it was so much more than a secure roof over her head, good food, books to read and games to play. It had just as much to do with the time they spent teaching her about the world around her and her place in it as a little girl who mattered a great deal to the people who loved her.

If he really was serious about coaching for the kids, Matt told himself, he needed to remember not every kid on his team was receiving the same attention away from the game. He remembered the commitment the coaching team had made to coach up the bottom third of the team. Luke, Mason, Gabe and Eli were the bottom third of the team in terms of their physical skills. But maybe Hunter, Ethan and Jermaine were the bottom third in the sense they had the physical skills but didn't yet have the emotional maturity to be great teammates.

He and the rest of the coaches had to earn their trust, and show them what a difference it could make if they really poured themselves into being part of the team.

After he and his wife tucked in Maelee for the night, Traci said, "I'm tired, too. I might read in bed for a while and see if I can doze off, if that's okay with you."

"Sure," he said, giving her a goodnight kiss. "I'm just going to work on an email to the parents."

Traci studied his face. "I never thought coaching a team would become such a big part of your life."

"Neither did I," he admitted. "But you know, if someday we might be trusting Maelee to some coach, we'll want it to be somebody who takes working with kids seriously."

Traci smiled. "Somebody just like you."

Matt shook his head. "Well, somebody just like I'm **trying** to be, anyway. I have a long way to go."

###

*Parents:*

*Hey folks! Trust you all are well.*

*I'm writing to let you know Coach Charlie will be leading a special drill Saturday before the game for anybody who wants to work on a couple of the key skills we're going to use as our secret weapons. So we hope your child can meet us at the ball park at ten o'clock Saturday for an extra hour of practice.*

*Your children are working hard and showing signs of real improvement. They look better on the field at every practice, and in every game.*

*Thanks for helping us encourage them by letting them know how well they're doing and how proud we all are of them.*

*Saturday will be a tough game and good test for the kids. We hope for a great turnout.*

*See you at the ballpark!*

*Coach Matt*

### 

Taylor, Brady, Gabe, Eli and Luke showed up. Not surprisingly, Hunter didn't. Matt thought about seeing the boy on Main Street trying to hang out with older kids, and being rejected. If only Hunter could be persuaded to pour that much effort into this team.

Charlie gave the five players who did show up thirty minutes of practice around things like dirt ball reads and tennis ball drop to improve their reaction time. He also coached them in making a delayed steal between second and third bases, and taking a secondary lead. Then B.J. led some bunting practice, including another round of competition, which all the kids enjoyed.

Afterward, Matt and Charlie agreed the kids were ready.

Matt watched as Luke and Taylor walked toward the edge of the ballpark. They stopped and talked for a minute. Then Luke ran back to the dugout, where Matt was packing up the equipment they had used.

"Hey, Coach?"

"What's up, Luke?"

"Well…you're not teaching me to pitch, and I bat almost last in the lineup. Am I ever gonna be good enough?"

Matt recognized a hint of belligerence in the boy's tone and knew the way he responded was critical. It could mean either gaining or losing trust in Luke's eyes. Matt also knew this was a test of his coaching commitments to be present, to be kind, and to coach them all.

Did he really believe that? Here was his chance to prove it. As he always did these days, Matt squatted and looked Luke squarely in the eyes. "Luke, do you trust me?"

Luke thought about it for a minute, then shrugged.

"Well, I want to earn your trust. And one way I'm going to do that is by always telling you the truth. Okay?" Matt pushed his ball cap back on his head, hoping Luke would look him in the eyes. "You are doing great Luke. You always work hard. You always pay attention. And all the players and coaches like and respect you because you're such a great teammate. You get that, right?"

"Yeah. I guess so."

"And because of that, you will get every opportunity to use what you are learning to become a real ballplayer. You just need to keep doing what you are doing, ok?"

Luke squinted as if he were giving Matt's explanation a lot of thought.

"Well I believe you will." He could see that Luke was still unconvinced. "And the other coaches know with practice, you'll continue to get better and better. But it isn't enough for the coaches to believe it. You have to believe it, too."

"I just need more practice?" asked Luke.

"We all need more practice, Luke. But here's what I *really* want you to know. This is more important than anything, okay? You're already good enough, for me, and all the other coaches. We care about you, Luke, unconditionally, and you don't have to catch or hit a single ball for it, just being you is good enough. We all love you just like you are buddy. I promise."

The hint of a smile began to steal across Luke's face.

### 

"What'd he say?" Taylor asked when Luke caught up to her and they resumed their walk home.

"He said I'm doing good and just need to keep working hard."

Taylor gave him a high five. "See! I told you!"

Luke grinned. "He said you and I should practice more."

"Really?"

"So can we come back after lunch? Will you help me?"

"Okay. Sure." Taylor pitched her glove into the air and caught it. Turning up the sidewalk to his house and promising to meet at the corner in one hour, Luke told himself he hadn't actually told a **fib** to Taylor. Coach hadn't exactly said to practice with Taylor, but he figured that was just a technicality.

### 

During the huddle up before the big game against the Screaming Eagles, the kids were psyched. Matt was nervous.

They reviewed their bunting and base-running strategies. They got their position assignments. They said their mantras.

*Small ball wins big games!*

*Put the ball in play and good things happen!*

*Fast to first, smart to home!*

The Screaming Eagles were bigger kids. They had better talent. Their record was 3-2, considerably better than the Bearcats' 1-4. Chances were slim to none Matt's ragtag team would send the Screaming Eagles home with a 3-3 record.

From the get-go, the Bearcats looked significantly better than they had before. They held the Screaming Eagles to one run in the first inning, who had two players in scoring position with only one out when Jermaine caught two fly balls to end the inning.

In the second inning, both teams scored once, for a score of 2-1.

In the third inning, Taylor struck out the first two batters and Zack got the third batter out unassisted after fielding a hard grounder down the first-base line. The Screaming Eagles seemed to think it was no biggie; the players showed no sign of discouragement when they took the field for the bottom of the third. After all, the Bearcats were cellar-dwellers.

*They think we're a joke,* Matt thought, *which means their coach thinks we're a joke.*

He'd been around sports long enough to know the coach set the tone for whether players respected their opponents, or ridiculed them.

"Way to play," Matt said as they trooped in from the field and prepared to bat. "Ethan, Hunter and Taylor, you're up. Watch me for the bunt sign. If you get on base be aggressive. He looked from Ethan to Hunter to Taylor. "You ready to play small ball?"

Before anyone could respond, Hunter said, "Hey Coach, I don't need a bunt to get around the bases. I can knock it outta the park."

Matt and Charlie exchanged glances.

"Hunter, we need baserunners, so let's do whatever it takes to make that happen. Remember, small ball—"

"I don't have to wait for a stupid girl to bunt."

Matt put his hand on Hunter's shoulder. "That's enough, Hunter."

The rest of the team grew quiet. Everybody knew by now what "that's enough" meant. It meant if you didn't stop whatever you were doing, you might have to sit out the game.

Ethan was up first, poked a solid line drive to left and made it to first with no trouble.

Then Hunter stalked up to the batter's box, his face set in a scowl. Matt knew this was not going to go according to plan. Matt gave him the bunt sign; the boy clearly saw him. Instead of following the signal, he took angry rips at three pitches in a row, striking out.

Hunter tossed his bat against the dugout when he walked past Taylor.

Taylor sacrificed and Ethan made it to second. With two outs and three players coming up who rarely got on base, it was as good a time as any to take a risk on the delayed steal Charlie had taught them Saturday.

On the second pitch to Luke, Ethan waited for the catcher to lob the ball back to the pitcher. When he saw the ball leave the catcher's hand, Ethan ran like crazy for third base and slide in safely.

The pitcher had his back to Ethan and didn't know anything unusual was going on until the crowd erupted.

The Bearcats' dugout was celebration central—the parents were on their feet cheering! Yelps of shock came from the other side of the field. The annoyed coach glared across the field at Matt. Matt tried to keep his smile friendly, not smug.

*Bearcats don't gloat,* he thought. *Except on the inside.*

Luke walked. Then Eli dribbled the ball down the first-base line and ran. He was small but fast. The Screaming Eagles first baseman stumbled to the ball as everyone on the Bearcats side rose to their feet screaming. Ethan broke towards home on the bunt and easily scored, tying the score at two. Luke had rounded second without hesitation and made it to third standing up.

Eli was safe at first.

"Nice job Luke! Great bunt Eli!" Matt called.

They still had two outs with runners on first and third.

Gabe was up to bat. He bunted fair but was out at first, stranding two players on base. But everyone was so excited no one seemed to mind. Matt almost got a lump in his throat watching them jumping up and down, hugging each other.

Everyone except Hunter.

They took the field to plenty of cheering from the stands.

In the next inning, the Screaming Eagles scored one run. In the bottom of the inning, Mason walked and made it to second after Jackson hit a solid ground ball to center field. Zack connected next with a grounder deep in the hole behind second base, beating out the throw to first, while Mason moved over to third and Jackson hustled safely to second. The bases were loaded. Once again, the players in the dugout and the people in the stands were on their feet.

Brady's high fly ball brought in Mason who tagged up from third. With one out Jermaine added a single to left center, driving in Jackson all the way from second. The score was 4-3, Bearcats.

Ethan walked to load the bases. Hunter struck out again and Taylor grounded out to end the inning.

By the final inning, the Screaming Eagles had tied the game at 4. *One run,* Matt thought. *That's all we need. One run.*

They went into the inning near the bottom of the line-up.

Gabe was up and with his tight strike zone, he drew a walk. Mason struck out. With a runner on base at the top of the order, lead-off batter Jackson came up with only one out. He passed on two balls and connected with the third for a foul. The fourth ball came straight across the plate and he hit a solid ground ball that whizzed past the center fielder. Gabe made it to third; Jackson coasted into second with a double.

Matt began to sweat. They had their first shot of the season to beat a team with a strong winning record.

Zack stepped up to the batter's box. Zack had proven to be their best player; focused and dependable. "Nobody better Zack!" he called out. "Just give us something hard and on the ground!"

Zack passed on a ball, then took a hack at the next one for his first strike. He fouled the next pitch. Strike two.

Matt's heart was pounding like crazy.

The next pitch was high and outside. Maybe the pitcher was getting as nervous as Matt. The pitcher kept glancing at Gabe and Jackson; clearly, their aggressive base running had rattled their opponent.

The next pitch was a ball. Full count.

Everyone on both sides seemed to be holding their breath. It was eerily quiet on the field.

Matt had played enough ball to recognize this as one of those moments when things seemed to be in slow motion.

The pitch was perfect; Zack squared it up. Clink! A frozen rope single to center field.

Gabe sprinted home. The game was over. With a final score of 5-4, the Bearcats were 2-4 on the season!

### 

Luke, like all the Bearcats, was having a hard time settling down after the win. They won! They beat the Screaming Eagles!

As soon as the coach got down on one knee, everybody quieted down to see what he had to say.

"We're so proud of you today," Matt said. "You did the little things right. You played like we practiced and, when we all do our jobs, good things happen." Then Matt gave each of the coaches a chance to say a few words about the game.

Beside Luke, Hunter kicked the dirt. Luke figured Hunter was still mad because he struck out twice.

"Today we gave ourselves a chance by working hard on a couple new skills that really helped us," Charlie said. "You should really be proud and enjoy this win; you earned every bit of it. We're going to continue to be the best bunters and base-runners we can be. It all started with the hard work you put into practice this week. Success is never an accident. When we practice hard during the week you see the results in the games. Outstanding job today, everybody came through when it mattered."

Then they broke the huddle by joining hands, counting to three and shouting, "Team!"

Walking home, Luke thought about everything the coaches had said. He was happy the Bearcats won. He was really happy Taylor and Gabe were stars of the game—two players who, like him, were kind of outsiders; Taylor because she was a girl and Gabe because he was still such a little guy. He figured if they could help the Bearcats win, so could he.

All he had to do was practice and get to be the best he could be.

### Coach's Rule #9

*Prepare the team by developing the skills and techniques that reinforce the game strategy.*

# CHAPTER 10:
# ...AND LOSING

With two games left before the playoffs, Matt's inclination was to launch into some kind of insane practice schedule, to push the kids to their limits. Funny how a small taste of success creates a hunger for more.

"It's like I keep forgetting they're ten years old," he told John as they walked with Buster along the greenway that connected Stonefield with the next little town down the highway. "But, you know, that last game against the Screaming Eagles, I still can't believe it. That was great."

John nodded. "You better believe it Matt. They're getting better. So winning a game isn't a fluke. It's what starts to happen when they get better."

"Okay. I get it. But we only have two more games before the playoffs—do I work them like crazy in practice?"

"Based on what I saw, you may have just enough time left for the magic to happen after all."

Matt made a face, "Huh?"

"Look, when a team is well led, they strive to do well not just for themselves, but also for their teammates. The kids feel safe. The kids are excited. They look forward to being together, even at practice. They understand the teams game strategy, and are confident because you fully prepared them on the right things. They play fast, loose, happy, and confident. When the kids come to believe that this is truly their team, and they make it their own, they become winners on multiple levels. These are special seasons that have an impact that can last a lifetime."

Matt stared off in the distance, "I can see it happening already. I see in practice. I saw in the game the other day. More than that, I can see it in their faces and hear it in their voices."

They paused while Buster nosed around a clump of early spring flowers emerging along the edge of the path. John said, "You want to win them over, you start with their eyes and their ears, and if you do right, you win their hearts and minds. You can tell when you get it right. Maybe you should keep doing what you're doing and don't freak the kids out by making these last two games more important than they are...just because you won a big game."

### 

When Hunter didn't show for the next practice, Matt knew he had to do something. If the boy didn't show up for practice and just disappeared from the team, Matt wouldn't have a chance to help him with anything. He felt strongly that he had to get Hunter re-engaged.

So after practice, Matt drove by Hunter's house. He knew he should have called, but he thought he'd try just driving by. Maybe he'd see the boy outside. Maybe it could seem like a casual encounter.

He realized as soon as he saw the address he didn't know as much about Hunter as he'd thought. Hunter's home was on the edge of town in a mobile home park—not one of the nicer parks, but a run-down area where times must be hard financially. The mobile home where Hunter lived was tidy and well-maintained, but not all of them were.

If he'd been asked, Matt would have assumed the kids on his team were from all walks of life. Some probably came from families with houses on the lake. Others were no doubt more like Matt's family, solidly middle-class. Clearly, making ends meet was harder for some than others. And Matt realized Hunter might have a chip on his shoulder. Hunter might feel the need to prove he belonged. Kids didn't know being different, or not having as much money or stuff as other kids, didn't mean they weren't as good. The chip on Hunter's shoulder, and his insistence on being the star of the team, now made a little more sense to Matt.

He kept driving.

Matt thought to himself, Hunter needs to understand he is an important part of the team, even if he isn't the star. And that was going to be tough if the boy didn't even show up for practice.

### 

Game day was hot, the hottest day of the season so far. And it was the last day of end-of-year testing at school, so Matt was pretty sure he could count on the fact most of the kids were tired.

And at least one of them—Hunter—was angry.

This could add up to a very bad formula: HALT (hot, angry, losing and tired). His kids had three of the four going for them already; he hoped this game would not fill in the only missing element in the formula—losing.

On the up side, they had momentum. They had won two of their last three games, and played pretty well in the one game they didn't win. Practice had gone well and the players were really looking good not only in the basics, but they were visibly bonding together as a team. On the down side, today they faced the Crushers, the team had earned their name. The best team in the league, they had only one loss on the season. Matt could tell just the thought of facing them intimidated his players. Heck, it intimidated *him*. Plenty of folks considered the Crushers' coach to be the best in the league.

How on earth did he prepare these kids for what would, without a doubt, be their toughest game of the season?

When they huddled up before the game, both the kids and the coaches were subdued. Matt knew they needed to hear something different today, something that had the chance to transform the next couple of hours from a potentially painful experience into one they could feel proud of.

As he got down on one knee to face his players, Matt didn't have a clue what he was going to say. After a few seconds of silence, during which the players riveted their attention on him, Matt asked quietly, "Are we better than we were a month ago?"

Most of the kids nodded.

"Are we?" he prodded.

"Yes!" chimed in Taylor and Luke and Eli.

"That's right. We're better than we were a month ago. You know why?"

They looked at him expectantly.

"Because today we're a team." A couple of the kids cocked their heads to one side and frowned. "A month ago, we had a team name and a team uniform. But you were just a bunch of kids who got together and tried to hit the ball and run around the bases. We didn't really know how to play together and support each other. Remember that?"

Most of the kids nodded. Every one of them—except Hunter—had their eyes on Matt.

"We practiced together and we ate popsicles together and we finally won a few games together. Along the way, something else happened that made us a team. You know what that was?"

Heads shook.

"I'll tell you what happened that really made us a team: We learned to care about each other."

Hunter actually rolled his eyes at that.

"Sometimes we still drop the ball. Sometimes we still strike out. And we wish we didn't. But being a team doesn't mean we get everything right. It means we care about each other even when we get things wrong." He paused, hoping he wasn't telling them something they were too young to understand. "Even if you drop the ball, your teammates still like you. Even if one person strikes out, we're still a team. That's what makes us a team."

Taylor was smiling. Luke had squared his shoulders. Eli was standing so straight he looked two inches taller.

"Even if one person drops the ball…" Matt stopped to let the team fill in the message.

"We're still a team!" came a half-dozen voices, if a bit tentatively.

"Even if one person strikes out…"

"We're still a team!" The response was a little more confident this time.

"And even if the Crushers win—"

"We're still a team!"

"That's right!" Matt affirmed.

"Now let's get out there and scratch out a couple of runs. Because that's what Bearcats do—we scratch!" He smiled and stood up. "What do Bearcats do?"

"We scratch!"

###

The game was brutal. As bad as Matt had dreaded it would be.

By the fourth inning, the score was 8-1, Crushers. They hit home runs. They hit high fly balls that seemed to attach themselves to the blinding sunlight overhead—fly balls nobody could even see, much less catch. They seemed to specialize in double plays and pitches nobody could hit. These kids were big and athletic and extremely well-coached. Matt had learned from Charlie after the Crushers finished the rec league season in a few weeks—finishing in first place—some of these kids would go on to play tournament ball during the summer, in a league that was well-funded and where they would travel around to play some of the best teams in the region.

The Bearcats weren't just losing, they were becoming discouraged.

The HALT formula—hot, angry, losing and tired—was complete.

As the top of the fourth inning drew to a close, Matt realized they were close to having the dreaded mercy rule come into play. The Bearcats hadn't lost a game by the mercy rule since the beginning of the season and he hated that it might happen now, especially given they had started what felt like a pretty good comeback.

At the top of the fifth inning, Jermaine managed a base hit.

When Ethan set up to bat, Matt took a few steps toward the on-deck circle, where Hunter was taking practice swings before his next at bat.

"Hunter, if Ethan gets on base, I want you to bunt."

Hunter hit the dirt with his bat. "No, Coach! I wanna get on base!"

"Hunter, we've been here before, haven't we? You could be the player who starts the rally," Matt pointed out.

Hunter made a face. "Coach, I can hit a home run! I don't wanna bunt!"

"The team just needs you to get your bat on the ball. If you do that—"

Matt heard the crack of Ethan's bat hitting the ball. As he turned to get back into his position on the first-base line, he said, "Bunt, Hunter. Start the rally. Let's go!"

Ethan's hit was a high fly, and the Crushers' outfielder dropped the ball for the first time in the game. Jermaine, who had been halfway to second base, sped up when the ball hit the ground and slid the rest of the way to safety.

"Hunter—"

The boy was already heading for the batter's box.

Before Hunter even took a swing at the ball, Matt knew the boy had no intention of bunting. He was a hot-headed kid with something to prove, and he was not going to make a play he perceived as taking one for the team.

Hunter swung for the fence.

The left fielder caught the fly ball. Jermaine remained on second, Ethan on first.

Hunter returned to the dugout and threw his batting helmet into the corner—an action that was expressly forbidden. Sarah Kate glanced at Matt to see how to handle it. But before either of them could react, Eli walked over to Hunter, gave him a friendly punch on the shoulder and said, "It's okay. We still like you."

Hunter froze. So did Matt and Sarah Kate.

"Shut up, squirt," Hunter said angrily.

"That's impolite," said Mason, one of the few times he had voluntarily interacted with another player except when the game called for it. "Eli was being nice and you were impolite."

"Yeah," Hunter said, "and you're just a freak, so you can shut up, too!"

Having heard the exchange, Taylor stopped on her way to the batter's box. Matt signaled her to get in the batter's box and strode over to the dugout.

"Hunter. Out!" He gestured the boy out of the dugout.

Hunter glared at Matt and seemed to be debating whether to defy him. Then he grabbed his ball cap and muscled his way through the dugout. Matt squatted by the gate and spoke in a low, calm voice. "Sit with your mother until this is over. Then I want to talk to you."

Hunter stared straight ahead.

"And while you're waiting, I want you to think about what Eli said. Because he's right."

Taylor struck out.

The players were subdued as they waited to take the field for the bottom of the fifth.

"Let's finish this strong, team," Matt said.

Taylor was sufficiently rattled she pitched four straight balls and walked the first batter, something she rarely did. Matt pulled her out, reminding her she'd pitched a good game and it was just time to take a rest. The second batter hit a hard ground ball to center field, which Brady managed to glove the ball in time to get the force out at second. The Crushers still had a player at first, with one out.

The third batter slammed a line drive into left field, where Eli managed to field it cleanly. He thought he had it in time to beat the runner heading to third, but his throw was short. With Luke fumbling the ball at third, the batter rounded first and was well on the way to second. Luke threw to second; the throw was off, and the ball bounced into right-center field.

The runner at third went home, and the runner at second advanced to third.

The Crushers had one out, a player on third and nine runs.

The bleachers behind the Crushers erupted in cheers.

The next player walked.

A hard grounder to right field brought in the player on third and moved the runner on first over to third. Two outs with the score at 10-1, Crushers.

Jermaine dug deep and delivered two good pitches. The batter kept popping fouls until he hit a line drive to right field. The runner on third scored—the game was over—mercy rule.

Hunter hadn't hung around.

### 

Matt sat in his truck long after everyone else had cleared out, feeling like an utter failure. Not because the Bearcats lost the game, but because he had lost Hunter. He kept reviewing all his interactions with the kid over the last few weeks, trying to figure out where he had gone wrong, what he could have done differently to help this troubled boy. After driving by Hunter's house, he had called three times but never got an answer or a call back.

A tap at the passenger window startled him. It was John. Matt rolled down the truck window.

"Got a fancy new coffeemaker for my fancy new kitchen," John said. "Run me home and I'll make you a cup."

They talked about everything on the drive to John's but the game. Even while they waited for the coffee, they continued their conversation about the turn toward hotter weather, a Sunday afternoon concert series on the town green, travel plans for the coming summer—John had none, Matt planned a long weekend at the beach with Traci and Maelee after the Bearcats' season ended. Only when they finally sat on the back deck with their coffee and looked out over the darkening woods did Matt finally speak about the one thing on his mind.

"I really messed up with Hunter."

"Did you?"

"Yeah. He went off on two of the other kids on the team. So I took him out of the game—out of the dugout. And he left."

"Sounds like the messing up might be on the boy."

"But I'm the coach. I should've managed it better. I should've been able to—"

"Able to what? Keep him happy? Save him from himself?"

"Why not? If a coach can't do that for a kid with a few problems, he's not much of a coach, is he?"

John shook his head dismissively. "A coach isn't a miracle worker. And he can't save every troubled kid who winds up on his team."

"I don't know, John…"

John leaned across the table in the near-dark to look him in the eyes. "You know why baseball is so good for kids? Do you?"

"It teaches them how to be part of a team. It teaches them hard work pays off. It teaches them sportsmanship."

"All that's secondary," replied John.

"Then what?" Matt asked.

"We talked about this before; It teaches them how to fail."

Matt frowned. "Well, my kids are sure learning that lesson this season."

"Good!" John raised his voice and pounded the table when he saw Matt's scornful expression. "I'm serious! Life is full of failure. Where's a kid going to learn to fail?"

"On my watch, apparently."

John's voice grew calm and quiet again. "Matt, here's one of the greatest gifts of kids' sports: It gives them a safe place to learn to fail. When you're telling those kids they need to like each other even if they drop the ball or strike out, you're teaching them it's okay to fail. That we all fail. Failure is the stepping stone to success."

*"Success is the end result of a series of corrected failures; successful people fail fast and move on."*

Matt was beginning to see John's point—up to a point. "But a kid like Hunter…"

"Right now, maybe Hunter's life might be full of failure. Maybe his dad's out of work; maybe his parents are divorced. I don't know. But whatever it is, his response has been to try and be the big shot, to try and get attention. That's because he believes he's the failure—not the circumstances of his life, but him. He's never had anyone teach him that failure doesn't mean he's worthless. He's never had a safe place to learn that having a failure doesn't mean being a failure."

"Okay. Yeah. That makes sense. But all I've managed to do is run him off."

"Holding him accountable for his behavior isn't running him off, Matt. You have to hold your kids accountable."

Frustrated, Matt shook his head. "This is too hard. Dealing with all these kids with their different problems, their different abilities. Dealing with their parents. I'm not sure it's worth it."

"Coaching is hard, no doubt about that. As for whether it's worth it, well, just wait till the end of the season, and take a look at Luke or Mason or Eli. That's when you'll get a glimpse of whether or not it's been worth it."

John relaxed into his chair, lowered his voice and smiled faintly. "But if you really want to know, check in with those kids in 20 years—that's when you'll be able to see what you really did for them."

## Coach's Rule #10

*Create a safe environment for kids to fail
and be okay. Success is the end result
of a series of corrected failures.*

# CHAPTER 11:
# TEAM FIRST

Luke was lying in the grassy infield with Taylor, Jermaine, Eli and Ethan, eating popsicles after practice.

"That was a good practice," Jermaine said. "I think we're gettin' pretty good."

"I just wish Mason would try to hit the ball," Ethan said.

"Yeah, but even if he doesn't…" Taylor said, then waited.

"...we're still a team!" came the cry from the other four, followed by giggles.

Luke was starting to feel like they really meant it, and not just when they said it about Mason, but about him, too. Something really did feel different from the way it felt in the beginning. Even after the Crushers crushed them last week, everybody seemed to be okay and even kind of happy—except for Hunter.

"I wish Hunter would come back," he said, not quite sure he meant to say it out loud until it was too late to take it back.

"Me, too," Jermaine said.

"Maybe we should go see him," Taylor said. "Tell him we want him to come back."

"I'm not telling him we still like him again," Eli said, and everybody laughed once more.

"I'm serious, though," Taylor said after the laughter died. "Maybe he just feels bad and thinks we don't like him anymore because he got mad and everything."

"She's right," Ethan said, sitting up and looking around. "He's just...I don't know...I think he's like me sometimes. He just wants to be a really good player, but it's hard to do what the coach says and stay dialed in. And, he has been striking out a lot."

"Sometimes I think he's sad," Luke said.

Nobody said anything for a moment, and Luke wondered if they were all thinking about his dad being dead and feeling sorry for him.

"Yeah," Taylor said, also sitting up and picking up their popsicle sticks. "But we're a team now. So it doesn't matter to us if he strikes out."

"Then we should go tell him," Eli said. "But I'm still not telling him we like him. He might pop me!"

They all laughed again and Jermaine threw his cap at Eli. Then they got up and ran around playing tag for a few more minutes before it was time to go home.

### 

Matt hurried down the aisle at the grocery store with a gallon of milk in one hand and a bunch of bananas in the other. Traci called him after his final job of the day to ask if he could pick up some things on his way home.

He was in the checkout line when an unfamiliar voice called out, "Hey, Coach!"

Turning toward the voice, Matt was surprised to see Tony, the Crushers' coach, coming toward him wearing a big smile. When Tony reached Matt, he said, "I just wanted to tell you how impressed I am by your team."

*What? Is he taking a shot at me?* Matt wondered. But the smile on Tony's face seemed genuine.

"I know they had a tough start to the season, but I can sure see the improvement," Tony continued. "A lot of people have. What really impresses me, though, is how much they seemed to hang together as a team. My kids, they're all ball players, but I don't see as much team spirit as I'd like."

"Thanks, Tony."

"Maybe I could buy you a cup of coffee sometime and we can talk coaching."

"Sure. Any time."

On the drive home, Matt couldn't stop thinking about the exchange with Tony, the most admired coach in the league. Everybody knew he had great athletes, but it also was a given he knew how to bring out the best in his players. Tony and the Crushers had been the talk of the league, two years in a row.

And here he was, talking to Matt like *he* knew a little something about coaching.

For a moment, the notion almost went to his head. Then it came to him: Tony was as good as he was because he had learned to be humble. Matt smiled. Another lesson for him to hang onto.

### ###

Matt was doing early set-up for the final game against the Terminators—a team named for a local NASCAR hero— when a player came walking slowly across the park toward the field.

It was Hunter.

Matt stopped unloading the bats, walked over to the bleachers and gestured for the boy to join him.

"I'm glad you came back, Hunter," he said.

Hunter shrugged, clearly a little embarrassed. "Yeah. That's what everybody said."

"Everybody?"

"The others. Ethan and Jermaine and Luke and Taylor." He stared at his feet. "Even Eli."

"You talked to them?"

Hunter nodded. "They came to see me. They…they wanted me to come back."

Matt felt the way he sometimes felt when he was overwhelmed by how happy Traci and Maelee made him. *These kids,* he thought, *did something I could never have done. They made him feel welcome enough to come back.*

"That's pretty cool," Matt said. "What did you think?"

"I told them you probably wanted me to stay away."

"I'm sorry that's how you felt, Hunter. That's not true."

"That's what they said. They said…they said the team needs me."

"They're right."

"So I thought, if it's okay, I'd play today, even though I missed practice this week."

"That's okay with me."

"Thanks, Coach."

"And Hunter?" Matt said as he dropped to one knee.

"Yeah, Coach?"

"I want you to think about what the other players said—the team needs you. It needs your leadership. You're a good player. That's what I wanted to tell you after the game last week. Hitting a home run or catching a fly ball isn't as important as being one of the players who cares about what's good for the team. That's what servant leadership is, you know, putting the needs of others first, and in this case that means your teammates. If you do, the benefits will always come back to you. *Play hard for your teammates and do whatever the team needs to be successful.* That's what my dad always said and that's how it always seems to work out for me."

Hunter nodded. "Okay."

"Wanna help me finish setting up?"

"Sure."

They stood and headed for the dugout.

"Coach?"

"Yes?"

"Thanks."

Matt nodded.

"Coach?"

Matt smiled. "Yes?"

"I'm...I'm sorry I was a butt."

Matt chuckled. "Did you apologize to Eli?"

"Yes, sir."

"Maybe you could apologize to Mason, too."

"Yes, sir." They worked together for a few minutes. Then Hunter added, "But he is kind of a dork."

Matt tried not to smile. There was no denying Mason was different.

"Well, Hunter, we all have things that make us different from each other. On our team, those differences make us the special team we are."

### 

Their opponent for the final game before the playoffs would be a tough one. Matt could only hope the Bearcats and the Terminators were more evenly matched, here at the end of the season, than they had been at the beginning.

Through the first five innings of this game, neither team had dominated but the Terminators managed to hold onto a slight lead.

The Bearcats made good plays early in the game. Ethan brought in two runs in the first to set the tone. Hunter at short stop made a diving catch for the final out in the second inning. Mason kept his eye on the runner at third base who kept taking a very long lead and turning his back to Mason when he returned to the bag. The third time the runner turned his back, Mason threw him out. The bleachers behind the Bearcats' dugout went crazy cheering for Mason and calling his name.

At the top of the final inning, the Terminators led by two runs.

With two good plays in the outfield by Jermaine and Hunter, the Terminators didn't add to their lead in the top of the sixth. The Bearcats needed three runs to win—and they'd never scored three runs in a single inning all season.

The bottom of the lineup was coming up.

Matt told himself a 6-4 loss in the final game to a team that was in the top half of the league was nothing to be ashamed of.

As they gathered in the dugout, Matt looked at Taylor, Luke and Gabe. "Put the ball in play."

"And good things happen!" the players shouted back at him.

"That's right. We need to scratch out three runs. That's all it takes. What do Bearcats do?"

"Bearcats scratch!" yelled the team.

"Okay! Let's make this happen."

Taylor, determined and all-business in the batter's box, hit a shot to right and made it safely to first base.

Luke, who had developed a good eye at the plate, waited patiently for a good pitch. After taking two balls, he fouled off the next two. On the next offering, Matt held his breath as Luke held off ball three for a full count.

Taylor, working her lead, got a good jump and stole second on the pitch.

People in the bleachers clamored for a base hit from Luke.

On a three-two pitch, Luke hit a bouncing ground ball to third. Instead of running into the tag, Taylor hedged at second. The third baseman fielded the ball cleanly and looked at Taylor, expecting her to run. When he realized she was not moving, he wheeled and threw to first.

As soon as the player threw to first, Taylor sprinted to third. The throw to first was late. Luke was safe on first and Taylor was safe on third.

Matt realized he'd been holding his breath the whole time. He told himself to start breathing.

Gabe was up. As small as he was, his strike zone was tight. Gabe passed on three balls. From the dugout, Hunter called, "Way to watch 'em, Gabe!"

On the fourth pitch—a strike—Luke successfully stole second base. Gabe had been taking all the way.

Glancing at Sarah Kate, her face beaming with pride, Matt told himself if the only good thing to come out of the season was a kid like Luke finding the confidence to steal a base, the season had been a good one.

The Bearcats had two players in scoring position, with no outs.

Gabe walked. The bases were loaded.

Mason came up to bat. This would be an easy out if this pitcher could throw strikes. Then they would be back at the top of the lineup.

The win was within reach.

When the first pitch came across the plate, something happened Matt wasn't expecting: Mason took a swing at the ball.

And missed.

Nevertheless, Matt was astonished. Mason had never once— not during practice, not during a game, not even when it represented their last out of the game—attempted to hit the ball.

The ball park was silent for a moment—Matt presumed everyone else was as shocked as he was.

Matt called out, "Good cut, Mason! You've got this!"

The second pitch was a ball, low and outside. Mason, as catcher, had developed a good eye and let it pass.

"Way to go, Mason," Charlie called out.

The rest of the spectators, even the kids in the dugout, were speechless.

The third pitch was outside for ball two.

The fourth pitch was a strike. Mason took another cut.

At that point, people in the bleachers began a low and steady cheer. "Ma-son! Ma-son! Ma-son!"

The fifth pitch was the third ball. Full count.

"Good eye!" Matt called.

Although no one had ever seen Mason make an attempt to hit the ball, Matt knew something had shifted for the boy. Unlike the past, when he intentionally let every pitch pass, Mason was reading the pitches. Matt knew in his gut what was happening.

The next pitch was a ball. Mason went to first and Taylor walked in.

The score was 6-5 with no outs.

After the cheering died and Jackson came up to the plate, Matt studied Mason on first base. Something amazing had just happened for a sharp kid who was differently-abled. Matt couldn't help but think of all the parents who had suggested to Sarah Kate—sometimes gently and sometimes angrily—that the boy did not belong on the team.

Jackson, who wielded a pretty good stick, was up next.

"Base hit, buddy," Matt called out.

The first pitch was inside; Jackson turned on it, ripping it down the third-base line. Just foul.

Matt called out a little more encouragement.

The second pitch was a ball. Jackson swung and missed for his second strike. At least he was up there to hit, Matt thought to himself, if you're gonna go down, go down swinging.

On first base, Mason, intently studying the pitches, was not ready to run. Matt heard him murmur, "That pitch was fast and low. Good pitch follows fast and low. Good time for a home run. Here it comes."

Intrigued to realize how closely Mason had been paying attention to the pitcher's patterns, Matt watched as indeed, the next pitch was perfect.

Jackson swung hard. Thwack! The metallic crack of the bat colliding with the ball told Matt this was going to be a rocket.

Everyone's eyes followed the ball.

Mason stood on first base, very still, calmly saying, "I believe this is a home run."

The ball sailed over the temporary fences set up in the outfield and into the weeds beyond. Jackson was on the way to first when Matt realized Mason was still standing on the base.

"Mason, run!" Matt called out.

"Okay. It is definitely a home run," Mason said, beginning a long, loose run around the bases.

The Bearcats' dugout went crazy as first Luke, then Gabe, then Mason crossed home plate. They all waited to high-five Jackson as he came across the plate. Matt trotted over, too. Despite the cheering from behind him, as Jackson came across home plate, Mason said in a very matter-of-fact way, "That was a very good home run."

### 

Matt got down on one knee as the Bearcats finally settled down and gathered for the end-of-game huddle.

"You've made a lot of people proud today," he said, taking a moment to look each player in the eyes. "Not just because you won this game—which was an awesome accomplishment—because you played your very best. You continue to improve every game and I could not be more excited for you."

He then took a couple of minutes to name some highlights of the game, being careful to mention each player on the team.

"Do you know what that proves?" he asked as he concluded the highlights. Everybody shook their heads. "It means every one of you contributed something special making it possible for the *team* to win. Now, anybody have something to add?"

Having exhausted themselves with cheering and congratulating each other before the huddle, no one said a word. Matt looked to the assistant coaches.

Charlie nodded and said, "Great win. Enjoy it. Let's get ready for the playoffs. See you at practice."

As the huddle began to break up, Hunter stopped and said, "Hey, Coach?"

"Yes, Hunter?"

"Thanks!"

## Coach's Rule #11

*Recognize each player has the potential to be a leader and make a contribution.*

| | BEARCATS | OPPONENTS | WIN/LOSS |
|---|---|---|---|
| GAME 1 | 2 | 9 | L |
| GAME 2 | 0 | 10 | L |
| GAME 3 | 1 | 11 | L |
| GAME 4 | 2 | 0 | W |
| GAME 5 | 4 | 8 | L |
| GAME 6 | 5 | 4 | W |
| GAME 7 | 1 | 11 | L |
| GAME 8 | 7 | 6 | W |
| | WINS | LOSSES | |
| OVERALL | 3 | 5 | |

# CHAPTER 12:
# THE BIG PAYOFF

Matt showed up at John's the next morning with fresh bagels from the bakery on Main Street. John was on the back deck, exactly where Matt had expected to find him, reading the morning paper with Buster snoring at his feet.

"Glad you came by," John said. "Congratulations are in order."

"Actually, this is more of a 'thank you' than a celebration," Matt said. "It's that, too. But mostly, I just wanted to tell you how much I appreciate what you did for me...and for the team. You're the unsung hero of the season."

"Bah! Get yourself some coffee and let's dig into these bagels," John said.

When Matt returned from the kitchen with a mug of coffee, he added, "We couldn't have done it without you."

"Well, you know what they say: When the student is ready, the teacher appears. I just showed up. You were the one who had to do the work. You and Charlie and the kids and the other coaches."

They savored the bagels, cream cheese and coffee, along with a blow-by-blow of the game.

"And Hunter came around," John said.

"He did. No thanks to me. A bunch of the kids on the team went to him, told him they wanted him to come back."

"No kidding?" John smiled. "That says you taught them something about leadership and being a team."

"So, John, how should we be thinking about the playoffs?"

"What do you think?" asked John.

Matt thought about it for a moment. "My granddad used to say, 'Dance with the one that brought you.' It was a long time before that made sense to me because, as far as I could tell, he didn't go to many dances. And I'd never been to a dance in my life. But I think I understand what it means for the Bearcats: Keep doing the things that work. Honor the commitments that we made to each other: players, coaches and parents. Work hard. Have fun. Be great teammates. Put others first. And be the best we can be on the last day of the season no matter what the scoreboard says when it's over."

"Okay, then. Go dance with the one that brought you. Buster and I will be there to cheer the team on."

As they finished breakfast and Matt prepared to leave, John said, "What if you make it to the championship game?"

Matt laughed. "That's not very likely."

John smiled. "You don't watch many baseball movies, do you? Don't you know the underdogs always win?"

"This isn't the movies, John. This is rec league baseball in a sleepy little town."

"Humor me. Suppose you do?"

"Okay. Then I guess we will play fast, loose, and happy, and leverage our advantages to win the game. And if for some reason we don't win, we've already won on so many levels with these kids the outcome in terms of the score of that game doesn't matter that much. Does it?"

John was grinning from ear to ear, and he added. "And what are your advantages?"

"Small ball...bunting and stealing. Right?"

"True. But your greatest advantage is your team culture. Like you said; fast, loose and happy kids which are energized and fully prepared. They practice hard, play for one another, and bring their very best effort to the game without worrying too much about making mistakes. When you get a group of kids to believe, and they own it, they are hard to beat. And that is your biggest advantage of all, Matt. Great job, coach."

All Matt could do was grin like an idiot.

### 

Rec league playoffs took place all in one day on the first Saturday in June, at the fancy new ball park where the highly competitive leagues played their regular season. The brackets were set and by late afternoon, two teams would finish a long, hot day competing for the rec league championship.

The Bearcats were impressed by the big ball park with its shiny brushed metal bleachers, the real concession stand selling hot dogs and snow cones, and the four different fields where eight teams could play at one time. Matt could see in their faces they were like a bunch of high school kids showing up on a big college campus to play for the state championship in front of thousands of people.

When they gathered for their first huddle, he asked, "This feels like a pretty big deal, huh?"

A couple of the kids nodded.

"I want you to remember something. The field is nothing. The bleachers are nothing. The fancy concession stand, nothing. There are only two things that can beat us now. The first thing is that team over there." He gestured to the other dugout. "They are just a bunch of ten year old kids, just like us, and we've already played them. They beat us early in the season, but if we play our game, we can take them. We're a much better team now than we have ever been. Agreed?"

The nodding was less tentative this time.

"They could beat us, but at this age, teams usually beat themselves. Pay attention to what is going on and stay engaged in the game." Matt tapped on his own forehead. "And keep the energy and effort high. You know what to do. Go out there and have fun!"

With enthusiasm, they swapped high fives and got ready for the first game.

They won the first game, then the second, knocking off two good teams. You could see their confidence build with each passing inning.

The Bearcats did not win either game easily. Along with making clutch plays in the field, the kids scrapped their way through by executing their game plan.

Clearly they believed they could play with anybody—and win.

Matt could not believe what he was witnessing, and on the very last day of the season.

In the end, they made it to the final game; the championship.

###

"Well, I sure never expected this," Will said when Matt pulled the coaches together after they realized they would play in the final game for the championship.

"I know. Me, neither," Sarah Kate said. "Do you think we can win it? I mean, really?"

All eyes turned to Matt. "Hey, somebody has to win it. Why not us?"

The final game would be another match-up with the Terminators. Matt was pretty sure the Terminators, after upsetting the Crushers, were not looking to let themselves be beaten again by the Bearcats.

He affirmed with his coaches that they'd stick to their plan. They were in it to win. Charlie, B.J., Will and Sarah Kate all agreed.

At the pre-game huddle, Matt got down on one knee, the way he always did now. All eyes turned expectantly to him. The kids were tired and dirty. It was hot. But they were also pumped up for the championship.

"Somebody's going to win this game—the whole shooting match—over the next hour and a half or so," he started. "Is there any reason it shouldn't be us?"

A few eyes grew very big.

"When we restarted the season, our goal was to be the best we could be by the last game of the season. And here we are, win or lose, this is it. Are you ready?"

Everyone nodded enthusiastically.

"We're playing a tough opponent. They hit the ball hard so we have to make plays. We've beaten them before, so we might as well plan to do it again. We don't have to save anything, because this is it. When it's over, it's over. Let's put everything we've got into this game."

The players were buzzing with excitement now.

Then he looked every player on the team straight in the eye before adding, "Remember—whatever happens, we've accomplished so much together, and we've already won our season. If we win, it's icing on the cake."

He looked at Charlie and nodded. Charlie said, "Let's go put some icing on that cake!"

This time, the Terminators did not take the lead and keep it. The lead bounced back and forth. Matt could not believe how evenly matched they were, with one team going ahead, then the other.

Going into the final inning, the score was tied at 5.

The Bearcats were up first and managed one run on a base hit by Hunter that advanced Taylor to third, who then stole home on a passed ball by the Terminators.

In the bottom of the sixth, the Terminators came to bat one run down. They were near the top of their lineup and the first batter quickly hit a high fly, which Hunter caught easily—a play he never could have made two months before. Taylor was tiring and it showed. She, Jermaine and Ethan had switched off pitching throughout the day. Jermaine had hurt his shoulder trying to slide into home plate in the previous game, so Taylor remained his best option to finish the game.

The Terminators' clean-up hitter singled down the third-base line, putting the tying runner on first with one out.

Taylor, digging deep, threw her best stuff to the next batter who swung at the first pitch and connected. Matt could tell by the sound it was well-hit.

It was a line shot into the right center field gap, rolling all the way to the fence. The hitter cruised into second with a stand-up double. The runner scored from first, tying the game.

Taylor battled the next batter, a lefty, to a full count.

On the payoff pitch, the left hander, protecting the plate, managed a looper off the end of the bat, which dropped in behind third base near the foul line.

From his left field position, Hunter got a good jump on the ball and fielded it on the second bounce. The runner who had been on second, seeing the ball down, was rounding third and heading for home. Hunter came up throwing and rifled a bullet towards home which Mason caught cleanly. While the play was well-executed, the tag was a little too late.

The ump signaled safe.

Game over. Terminators 7. Bearcats 6.

As the game ended, the Terminators received their share of cheers.

As the Bearcats made their way toward their dugout, exhilarated despite the loss, they found dozens of players and parents from other teams had stuck around for the championship game. They were giving the Bearcats a standing ovation. Matt saw Traci standing by the fence clapping enthusiastically, with Maelee in her stroller. John stood in the bleachers cheering, and even Buster looked excited for a change.

Matt was momentarily disappointed, mostly because he expected his players to feel bad about the loss. But he realized, amid all the cheering and applause, his team was in high spirits. They were hot, dirty, and exhausted, but they were grinning from ear to ear.

The players were celebrating almost as if they won the season. Because, of course, they had.

When they finally quieted down, Matt squatted with his kids. "I'm so proud of every single one of you. I never could have imagined you could make such a turnaround and get so much better in a few short weeks. You're amazing, and I'll always be proud of you."

"I have a few important things to tell you," he continued. "First, Will just informed me that Taylor and Zack have been selected for the All-Star team."

Cheers erupted. Taylor, as tired as she was, jumped up and down in excitement. Zack took high fives from everyone.

"That's a really big deal and reflects positively on our entire Bearcats team," Matt said. "It's also a really big deal because

Taylor will be the first girl ever to play on this division's All-Star team."

More cheers. Luke, in particular, was excited over the announcement about his friend.

"But what I want to leave you with is something that's more important than winning and losing or even All-Star teams," Matt said. "We've made lasting friendships we can carry into middle school and beyond. We've grown to respect people who are different, while accepting one another. We've learned about leadership and when and how to use our talents to serve the rest of the team. All these things—these lessons—can change our lives. That's what we did here this season that's really important." Matt knew he was talking to himself as much as he was to the kids.

"And there is no doubt that we played absolutely positively the best we have ever played, today, on the very last day of the season. And in the championship game no less!"

"Give yourselves a big hand."

He started clapping his hands and soon everyone joined in enthusiastically, including the parents. Matt even saw a few damp eyes in the crowd.

When the applause died down, Matt was ready to send them home one last time when Sarah Kate stepped forward.

"Before everybody takes off, there's a couple of other things to cover," she said. "Coach Matt's apparently too humble to tell you this, but he has been asked to coach the All-Stars." There was more applause, accompanied by congratulations and back-slapping, all of it a little embarrassing for Matt. He had been stunned to learn Tony, the Crushers' coach, had recommended him.

"And finally," Sarah Kate said, "the players have a little something for Coach Matt."

All the players had really big smiles when Mason stepped forward with a big, shiny gift bag covered with images of baseball bats and gloves. Awkwardly, Mason thrust the bag at Matt and said, "Here. This is from us. We made it."

Matt took the bag. Inside was a plaque made entirely of popsicle sticks. At the center of the plaque was a collage of Sarah Kate's photos from throughout the season. Across the bottom was the date and at the top it simply said, "Thanks, Coach Matt." Each of the kids had signed one of the popsicle sticks.

### 

Matt sat in the dugout after everyone left, feeling better than he could have imagined as he stared at the plaque the kids— *his kids*—had made for him.

He was so lost in thought he was startled when John and Buster came up behind him.

"Bet you never expected this, did you?" John asked.

"No. No, I can honestly say, I never expected to be this happy. Especially the way this season started." Matt shook his head. "I thought this was just a game. I never realized this was about more than baseball. It's about having an impact on their lives."

"That's right. Their lives, the parents lives, the coaches lives, and yours too, Matt. You did good, son," said John, laying a hand on his shoulder.

Matt looked up into the old man's eyes and saw pride there. The same kind of pride he'd felt when he looked at his team a few minutes ago.

About that time, they both heard a voice from the direction of the parking lot behind them.

***"Hey, Coach!"***

Matt turned. It was Luke, running up to him with something else in his hands.

"Hey, buddy. What's up?"

"Just…I just had something else. For you."

With that, Luke thrust an envelope into Matt's hands and immediately turned to run back toward the parking lot.

Scrawled across the front of the blue envelope in the young boy's awkward handwriting were the words, "Coach Matt." Inside was a Father's Day card, signed by Luke.

## Coach's Rule #12

*It's not how you start, it's how you finish.*
*Work with what you have, and*
*make it great for everyone.*

# EXTRA INNINGS

# COACHES' RULES

### Rule #1
*Answer this question first: "Why am **I** doing this?"*

### Rule #2
*Do it for the kids, not the parents, not for the love of the sport, and not for your own ego.*
*It's about the kids—all of them.*

### Rule #3
*Define clear expectations for players, coaches and parents; otherwise, a team's culture develops by default.*

### Rule #4
*Build a team of volunteers who have skills that complement yours, who share your passion and enthusiasm, and who align with your vision for the team.*

### Rule #5
*Create a vision of success with multiple outcomes, some of which are totally within YOUR control, so the season can be a memorable success, even if the team's win column falls short. Ultimately, this is how you win on the scoreboard too.*

### Rule #6
*Set the tone and take the lead in establishing team culture for the players, coaches and parents.*
*Know the coach is the coach.*

### Rule #7
*Establish language that reinforces the
program, and speak it often.*

### Rule #8
*Define multiple measures of success
around outcomes you control.*

### Rule #9
*Prepare the team by developing the skills and
techniques that reinforce the game strategy.*

### Rule #10
*Create a safe environment for kids to fail
and be okay. Success is the end result
of a series of correct failures.*

### Rule #11
*Recognize each player has the potential
to be a leader and make a contribution.*

### *Rule #12*
*It's not how you start, it's how you finish.
Work with what you have, and
make it great for everyone.*

# AFTERWARD

This book was written for one reason. The kids. All of them.

While wrapping up this book in the spring of 2015, I attended a day-long event with a group of successful business leaders. The facilitator posed the following question:

"Other than a family member, what individual has made the greatest impact in your life…and why?"

More than half of these executives recalled a childhood coach. Not just the coach's name, they shared in detail exactly the words the coach had spoken to them, how they felt, and how those words remained with them over the years.

Coaches profoundly impact peoples' lives. The opportunity to coach is a privilege and significant responsibility.

And "Hey, Coach!", thanks for stepping up!

# ABOUT THE AUTHOR

Jeff Dudan is a successful entrepreneur and founder of AdvantaClean, a franchisor of light environmental services.

He delivers leadership lessons learned through years of coaching youth sports and building an international franchise organization that help people in the workplace, coaches and *you* "connect the dots".

Jeff is a passionate servant leader in both business and athletics and has coached over 30 unique teams of youth athletes of all ages in football, basketball, and baseball.

This experience taught Jeff the influential role coaches play in early childhood development. His mission is to share the lessons learned so that coaches of all types can provide a memorable and positive experience for all those they lead, both on and off the field.

Jeff grew up in Schaumburg, Illinois, participating extensively in youth athletics, ultimately completing his career as a football player for Appalachian State University.

His journey as an entrepreneur began during college when he founded a summer business painting student housing, quickly becoming the largest painter town. In 1994, Jeff founded the company which would one day become AdvantaClean, expanding rapidly into hundreds of franchised locations.

Jeff is a life-long learner who exists to serve others by connecting dots and challenging them to be the very best they can be on the last day of the season, whenever that might be for them.

# ACKNOWLEDGMENTS

If we lose our why, we lose our way.

My purpose and inspiration are my wife Traci and courageous kids Zack, Maelee, and Jackson.

Always a tough out…there's nobody better.

Mom, Dad, Rusty, Pickle, Grandma Red, Vic, Mae and Leo. All of the nieces, nephews, and in-laws.

Players, parents and coaches of the past, present and future. Luby. Zerfoss.

Peg Robarchek, editor and co-conspirator on all things Stonefield.

AdvantaClean Nation, all of us, together.

23360511R00126

Made in the USA
Middletown, DE
23 August 2015